ALIENS' SACRIFICE

A REVERSE HAREM SCI-FI ROMANCE

CADY AUSTIN

Reazus Prime is a hard planet. Once a prison, it was abandoned when the mines dried up and the Overlords could no longer turn a profit off the prisoners. Now it's a haven for outlaws, pirates, and anyone holding a grudge against authority.

It's isolated, alone, and the only ships coming are the worst sort. One such ship carrying a cargo of abducted human women, explodes in orbit. A lucky few were ejected in pods, only to crash on the outlaw planet.

Now the race is on to find and claim the human females.

1

Giving the aliens the bird didn't do much—they probably didn't even understand it—but it sure as hell felt good.

The aliens standing on the shoreline watched as the waves took me deeper out. At least my impromptu boat ride got me away from *them*. The creepy beings had huge skulls and tiny teeth that were jagged and horrible like a piranha's. Seeing their red eyes peering at me was a nightmare come to life when I found myself rudely yanked out of my stasis pod. Now, after forcing a gallon of some gross drink down my throat, they had pushed me into the freaking ocean.

Angry all over again, I turned around, nearly pitching myself out of my stasis pod-turned-boat and into the choppy waters, and flipped them another bird. Huffing when they didn't react, the creepy little assholes, I flung myself back onto the floor of the pod.

How the hell had I gotten from California to *here*?

The little green men were unforgettable. Disoriented, I almost hadn't believed my eyes when I woke up on a spaceship and found a bunch peering at me and several other women. We were in what seemed to be a spaceship, and the green men had ignored us crying or trying to attack them, instead stabbing us with needles and forcing us to swallow nasty, bitter things. Somehow in all the injections, I understood their garbled language.

Abducted from Earth by little green men. Now all I had to my name was this stasis pod they'd shoved me in. I didn't even know how I landed on this planet. Had the green aliens dropped me off like trash? And where were the other women?

The choppy water splashed at the edges of my stasis pod. It was amazing I even knew what a stasis pod was, followed by actually being stuffed inside one by aliens. A regular woman like me, a verified taxi driver, finding out those sci-fi movies actually had things right on occasion?

Nuts.

But I wasn't sure my stasis pod, an egg-shaped shell with a hard bed in the center, was built to be a boat. Every little wave hitting the pod made me cling to the edge, knowing my jeans and hoodie would only make me sink. That, and being the only girl at the beach who didn't know how to swim...

Why hadn't I learned to swim?

The sound of drum beats made me look over my shoulder. The gangly aliens bounced on the beach around drums now, the sound echoing out over the arid landscape with a chilling effect. It felt like being in the middle of a nature documentary: the kind where the natives liked the taste of human meat.

One alien wearing dark green robes with gold chains around his throat stepped up to the edge of the water and called out.

"Great Monster! We beseech you to accept our offering!"

"Offering?" I yelped, sliding on my feet as I attempted to stand. I shouted back at the shore, "Are you *sacrificing* me?"

The lead alien in charge of whatever messed up ritual this was ignored me. I was just the sacrifice, after all. Cupping his hands around his mouth, he shouted, "Great Monster, heed our call! Bring us good weather and abundant tithes from the land!"

Great. So sacrificing me was the alien version of a rain dance.

My pod had drifted quite far from the shore now. The two suns glinted off the water like thousands of glittering blades. I gulped. Was that a shadow?

There couldn't actually *be* a monster under here... right?

Another shadow disabused any of those hopeful thoughts. Something large *was* under the water. Swimming in circles around and around, making me dizzy as I tried to follow it. Tugging at the top of the stasis pod didn't work. Not only was the hinge broken from where the stupid aliens back there had destroyed it, but closing myself inside the pod, if it even protected me from this thing, would probably just make me drown quicker once it submerged.

A splash made me shriek. Ice cold water drenched me the next instant. I gasped, spitting out the salty water as my pod careened wildly from side to side. Bracing myself was a losing battle. I banged my head against the side of the pod and spread my arms, holding on as the pod tipped almost totally on its side.

On the shore, the aliens hooted and hollered.

The monster was here.

"Assholes!"

What did I have? Well, beyond my good looks that couldn't keep a man, I basically had my hoodie strings to use as a weapon. Perfect - I could strangle myself on the way down this thing's gullet.

A horrendous smell slapped me in the face, like a thousand tuna fish dinners rotting on a Florida beach. As I gagged, something slimy and pink and decidedly *tentacley* curled over the edge of the pod right by my nose.

A literal sea monster.

Hyperventilating wasn't an option. As another tentacle rose into view, waving in a menacing way over the top of the pod, I gulped. Neither was jumping in the water. Drowning versus being eaten by a freaking alien kraken.

"It's not going to rain because you *kill me!*" I shouted toward the shore. The aliens kept dancing.

I huddled back down, biting my tongue on another scream as the pod lurched in the choppy water, the freezing water splashing me as a reminder of how deadly the water was in other ways. The kraken was antsy for its midmorning snack and if it didn't get me, hypothermia might. Huddled down, I shivered and tried to rub some warmth into my frozen arms.

Not lookin' good, Nat. Not at all.

My options were pretty much be eaten and die, or drown and die. Oh, and increasingly, freeze and die.

Tears streamed down my face. I wasn't supposed to be here. I drove a cab! Right now, I should be getting chewed out by my boss or ignoring some creep in the backseat who thought telling me he was a director was a hot ticket to my pants. Krakens were *not* in the picture!

A tentacle flopped to the bottom of the pod on the other side of me. Gasping, I jerked away, but another tentacle stopped me. There were five coming over the edges now. If I didn't dive into the water, *it* was coming for me.

Praying this was a dream wouldn't help. But facing that these might be my last moments alive was a hard pill to swallow.

A flash of searing blue light overhead made me cry out in alarm. What *now*?!

"The weaponsmiths! Shoot the thieves from the air!"

I glanced back in alarm to find the aliens scurrying around on the shore, finding their weapons. Several spears flew out toward the water, thrown impossibly far and high. Impossible for beings with tiny arms like those—but again, I didn't know anything about the world I was dropped into. Super strength could have been normal here. Only a few of the spears landed near me, more than two hundred yards from the shore, causing tiny splashes as they hit the water.

I perked up. Maybe this was a good thing. Let them kill the kraken and I could get out of here. Somehow.

"I've *got* to learn how to swim," I muttered.

The thing in the sky drew my attention. All of the spears missed the streak of light and it seemed to almost tease the cultist aliens. Diving, swooping, and circling in the sky, it looked like it was having a blast while the aliens on the shore howled in impotent rage.

But the light show hadn't taken my attention for long. The horrifying smell grew as a giant tentacle slid over the top of the pod. I ducked down, holding my breath as the thing's smell overwhelmed me. The tentacle was covered with an endless amount of tiny suckers, all of them pulsing in the air as if trying to reach out for its prey.

Another tentacle slid over the edge of the pod, small and heading directly for me.

I scrambled back as much as I could, shoes slipping on the slick surface. "No-no-no-no-no."

The end of it found my shoe. I kicked, but the wriggling tentacle slid upward and wrapped around my ankle. The suckers pulsated on my skin and it immediately wrapped another loop around me. Despite how I kicked, there was no escaping it. Even trying to pry it off with my hands didn't work. It was like trying to pry off a cement boot.

"Get *off*!"

Tears stung my eyes and blurred my vision. I kicked at the tentacle with my free foot and only managed to make hot pain burst in my ankle. The Lovecraftian creature had tentacles made of freaking stone! Stuttering in pain and fear, I kept trying to yank my foot free, but every time I did, it ended up coiling another loop around me.

By the time I looked up, tentacles covered my calf all the way to my knee.

BAM!

Light starburst overhead and even in my frantic struggle, I

noticed. My head tilted back and I gawked at the streak of light that had become more distinct as it hovered overhead. Little green men, I understood. Even the creeps back there on the shore, I understood. Them, I could wrap my head around.

But I didn't understand the giant silver Hulk flying through the air.

"Ah!" My attention returned to the kraken which had decided to exert more of its strength. It yanked me across the wet side of the pod, so hard my head jerked back and hit the wall with a nasty thump. No more resistance in the way, it lifted my leg over the side of the pod and tried to pull me into the water.

My fingers scrabbled at the floor, but it was some smooth surface. There was no hope of a handhold there. The only hope I had was grabbing the edge of the pod as it dragged me over... but that meant being dragged over.

I was going to die.

"—see your little pet dead!"

I didn't have more time to gawk because right then, the kraken suddenly lifted me into the air by my ankle.

With the shrieking cries of the cultists on the shore, the kraken yanked me away from the last safe harbor I knew.

2

I wasn't scared of much.

Bugs didn't creep me out. Snakes didn't give me hives. Even as a kid, being scared of a boogie man hiding under my bed didn't occur to me.

But the water?

My worst nightmares were populated with dark shadows circling under the water. Shark Week on TV made me scramble to cover my eyes like slasher movies never did.

Now a massive, tentacled monster swung me wildly in the air by my ankle.

In between brief periods of clear sight of the water, I glimpsed a whole mass of wriggling tentacles churning underneath the waves. My screams split the air as it wiggled me above the writhing mass.

But the chances of Death by Kraken went down with each spear thrown past me while the chance of being stabbed in the gut went up. Another rushed by my head, nearly taking off a chunk of my hair. The aliens on the beach were too far away to hear distinctly, but they shrieked in dismay and used their own spears to smack who I thought had thrown the spear. Their kraken friend wanted its food to wriggle and didn't want me a shishkabob.

Flailing around, trying to get my leg out of its hold was no use. I'd just drown or be caught by the mass of tentacles waiting below.

Then water surged up and I went flying higher in the air. In turn, I clung to the tentacle gripping me, screaming. I needn't worry about being lunch anymore. A drop from this height would be instant death. Kicking and struggling would only make that likelihood increase. Various expletives left my mouth instead as I clung to the massive tentacle supporting me.

The reason for this shift wasn't evident at once, but after a moment when I had my balance again and could stomach looking at the water, I saw why the kraken had reacted as it had. Blue-white arcs of electricity attacked the tentacles closest to the water and the base of the tentacle holding me. I couldn't tell where they came from, but it spanned in a wide circle around us.

If the kraken dropped me, I would've been electrocuted *then* drowned.

Perfect.

"Hold on!"

The shout came from behind me. I awkwardly turned and found the giant man hovering at eye level with me on some sort of flying paddleboard. Silver Hulk. Up close, a ragged scar bisected his right cheek and unnerving white eyes more stared at me as if seeing a vision.

"Thanks!" I shouted over the roar of the churning water below. "Hadn't thought about that!"

But my voice was lost in the roar of the paddleboard. Sparks shot from the backend of it and he looked past me grimly and tilted the board down and zipped away, becoming a silver streak in the air. Following him made my eyes tear up and I blinked, clearing away the pale afterimages burned into my sight, opening them again to find him swinging a giant two-handed sword toward a huge tentacle as it burst through the water.

That sword was taller than me. And it cleaved the massive tentacle in two before it could even reach him.

Maybe snarking at him was a bad idea.

More tentacles lashed out. Flailing and twisting as the kraken searched blindly for the enemy hurting it. One tentacle the thickness of my thigh caught the edge of the paddleboard. Silver Hulk nearly tipped over the edge and into that writhing mass, but caught himself and snarled. His next swing took out two of the tentacles at once.

The world lurched. I closed my eyes and tried to hold onto the thin thread of my sanity—and my stomach contents. The smell of nasty, rotted fish intensified. The rush of water pouring off the giant, writhing mass nearly overwhelmed the roar of the flying paddleboard.

The kraken lifted itself out of the water.

The stench made me gag and vomit rose to the back of my throat, foul and acidic. At the same time, however, I realized the kraken had looped its tentacle around my middle. My vision exploded with stars as it squeezed me and then dimmed to black at the edges. It was pain but beyond pain, an endless pressure on my heart and lungs. So this was what losing consciousness felt like.

Head falling forward, I slumped.

It felt natural, the way I fell. Through the air, wind whipping at my hair and clothes. Then a groan as something hit me hard, with all the force of a brick thrown off a skyscraper. The tentacle around my middle disappeared and strong arms pulled me against a naked chest. I slowly opened my eyes, my whole body throbbing dully. Something was wrong in my midsection but I ignored it for the moment as I looked into Silver Hulk's unsettling, yet kind eyes.

In a metallic voice, he said, "We got you."

Except he didn't. The next instant, I was allowed to slide

down his body until I gripped his kneecap, huddled at his feet. The alien turned and used the flat edge of his weapon to smack a reaching tentacle. "Get back, you foul fish!"

The cultists on the shore were going nuts with this development. I regained my senses enough to peer over the edge of the paddleboard. There was a lot of kraken blood in the water.

The silver alien continued giving it a beating above me, the huge weapon singing in the air. More foul, dark blood oozed to the water below and the cultists' rage was real.

More and more spears were sent, now seemingly without care of hitting me as long as one hit Silver Hulk.

Above me, as spears whirred by the paddleboard, getting closer and closer each time, the alien said, "We should get out of here. We've done enough damage."

The alien answered itself. "I agree. Before those idiots feed us to their pet."

The leg I clung to tried to move. Above, the alien said, "I can't shake her off."

"Leave her," he replied to himself.

I didn't have the energy to figure out why the Silver Hulk was talking to himself. And *answering* himself. Closing my eyes, I kept my mouth firmly shut on the bile wanting to fill my mouth as the alien pointed the paddleboard away and we glided off. I gripped his leg like the lifevest it was. The wind tugged at my hair, bringing more of the kraken's gag-worthy scent to me.

A spear thunked into the paddleboard. It swung wildly underneath me and the Silver Hulk compensated, leaning forward to stop the paddleboard from throwing us into the water. I figured the crazy, untranslated words exploding from his mouth were expletives. They sure escaped from me, especially when one wild swing had me swinging over the edge of the paddleboard and staring at the water.

The kraken's shadow went on forever. Half the ocean was made up of it.

I squeezed my eyes shut just as the alien righted us. He set us on course for the shore far away from the cultists and their spears.

We landed on the shore. I fell off the paddleboard, landing on my back on the cool sand.

"Did you kill it?" My voice came out in a croak.

"Impossible," the alien said in his strange metallic voice. "That relic is over a thousand years old."

"A pity we lost the pod." With my eyes still closed, this time I noticed a difference in his voice when he started to speak to himself. It was subtle, but not as metallic.

"At least we angered the Moxic some."

"Not nearly what they deserve."

I peeled open one eye and then the other. Silver Hulk glared across the distance toward the cultists.

"Are you talking to yourself?"

He looked down at me, a giant observing the tiny mouse at his feet.

"No," he said, "but in a way, yes."

He turned his back and knelt on the ground on one knee. Sitting up on my elbow, my fascination with him turned to alarm as his bare back started... *morphing*. Holy shit! I sat there gaping as the dude came apart, skin splitting like a candybar wrapper. My stomach churned and I could've been sick for a whole new reason as his body did something nobody... no *body* should have been able to do.

My hand curled in the coarse dirt, grounding myself. This was reality. Reality where this guy was morphing, skin and bone and guts splitting into... into...

No one would blame me for checking out a little.

When my vision returned, my faculties swooping back in at the last minute, three silver men stood before me.

One giant.

Three men.

"W-what... was that normal?"

The three men were similar enough to be triplets, though there were some noticeable differences. Their jawlines were different, and one had obviously broken his nose in the past. The guy who looked back at my question had a scar bisecting his cheek, the tip of it ending just below his eyelid.

"Yes," he said. Gone was the metallic, robotic voice. His voice was husky, better suited to the bedroom with its low notes, making my spine tingle.

"Oh. Ahem." My cheeks heated. So I had a thing for voices.

"We can salvage some of this," said another one as he picked up the paddleboard and frowned at the motor on the back.

The other alien squinted back toward where we had come. "Is it functional now?"

He grimaced. "For a short time." A spear embedded itself into the sand a foot from the one with the paddleboard. He considered it. "Hmm... maybe I'll look at this later."

"That would be preferable," said the other in the same deadpan voice.

The one with the scar crossed to me. "Can you walk?"

"I think—ah!"

He put his hands under my ass and back, lifting me up so smoothly I felt the rush of air before I felt his hands on me. I gulped as I looked into his face, noting the gray eyelashes and gray hair clipped close to his scalp. He smirked and a devious light entered his eyes. "Find something you like?"

"Um..."

"Anytime now, Arctok," called one of the others.

"Arctok? Is that your name?" I asked as he carried me back to the paddleboard.

"Feel free to say it anytime," he said. In that 1950's bedroom voice, I had a hard time imagining *not* growing a little damp.

"Anxious little thieves, aren't they?" said one of them up

ahead. "Let's get airborne and as far as possible. We can't afford another fight so soon."

Suddenly, Arctok looked down at me as he stepped behind the others onto the paddleboard, scrutinizing me as if seeing me for the first time. "You did *want* to be rescued, right?"

One of the others scoffed. "Yes, I'm sure becoming chow for their pet is her idea of exploring the universe."

"Well, *I* wouldn't assume," Arctok said. The noise from the cultists was growing louder. A glance over my shoulder showed them on foot, but coming fast, their long, skinny legs eating up the sand between us, their snarling faces confirming the fact they didn't plan to bring me a towel and umbrella.

I bobbed my head, hands tightening on Arctok's shoulders —broad, broad shoulders. "Definitely needed rescue. Thanks."

The alien in front sniffed. "Too bad about the pod."

The engine roared to life and Arctok shifted underneath me, smoothly flowing into a better stance for flying on a huge paddleboard while the other two repositioned themselves similarly.

With a howl of outrage from the cultists, we were off.

3

There wasn't anything better than being carried around in the arms of a hot, seriously buff dude. Oh wait. *Unless* you were flying through the air and you had to cling to the buff dude and dream of better days, like seatbelts on commercial flights. Even the scenery became just a blur to me as I focused on things like not hyperventilating.

"This thing has too many hits!" called the guy in front. My eyes teared from our speed, my hair whipping over Arctok's shoulder as we careened over trees. There were forests as far as I could see. "We better put down soon before this piece of junk puts us down!"

The other's voice was calm as he answered. "As far as we can go, Terono."

The wind was getting to me. Even my hoodie wasn't holding up and my shivers were now unbearable. My soaked clothes weren't helping. Arctok's body heat was insane, but not enough with the wind constantly hitting us. I curled into him more anyway, not even ashamed of how wiggling into his bare chest might seem. My hands were too cold to even feel a hint of embarrassment.

Luckily, we were headed for the ground. The driver navigated through the trees and found a small clearing where we could land. Arctok let me go and I stumbled to the ground, debating kissing it before Arctok grabbed my arm so I didn't fall face first to the forest floor.

"Are you injured?"

"No," I said in the same instant I put my weight on my ankle. I winced. "Maybe."

Kicking the kraken hadn't been the best idea. Now my ankle was angry and felt swollen too. Arctok helped me sit down and I collapsed in a shivering, hurting heap. Putting my head between my knees felt like a good idea, so I did it.

"Just a driver," I murmured to myself. "I'm never eating sushi again."

"Kron, do you have the wrapping tape? The human's leg looks to be injured."

I looked up to see the alien who'd been the calmest so far look over to me. He nodded and removed a roll from one of the many pockets in his pants. "Here," he said. He handed what looked at first glance like a disposable tampon container over top of the other alien who was muttering over the paddle-board's engine. "Terono, food first, then salvage."

"We're a good distance away," Arctok said as he crossed to me, kneeling down in front of my legs. "We should've lost the Moxic."

"For a time," Kron said.

Terono agreed. "They have our tech. If they've figured out how to use it, they can track us easily."

"They're idiots," Arctok said with a bark of laughter. "They couldn't tell a tracker from their dicks."

The tampon holder turned out to be a flexible tape dispenser. Arctok grabbed the side of it and pulled out a thin, black piece of tape that turned out to be reflective. I forced my frozen fingers to unstick and rolled up the leg of my jeans.

"Your shoes too." With an assessing glance, he said, "You're soaked. You may as well remove everything. Your clothes will need to be dried."

My teeth chattered and I couldn't answer. He took my teeth chattering as my answer and pulled my ankle into his lap. He removed my sock and I tried not to find it sexy how he ran his finger softly over the top of my arch. The cold had infiltrated me so thoroughly, I barely felt it anyway.

He secured the tape around my ankle and the black, reflective material winked in the dying sunlight as Arctok pulled back. I wasn't one to deny a helping hand, so I gratefully let him help me stand up. Testing out my ankle, I found it stiff, but there wasn't as much pain when I tried to put weight on it.

"T-t-thanks," I chattered.

Terono crossed to us and handed me a bundle. "Here," he said. "It stinks of fish but it's usable. It was stowed near the engine so it'll be warm enough."

I took it and found an extra large shirt that was obviously one of theirs. The fish smell *was* potent but the shirt was toasty warm and dry. I gave him a shaky smile. "Thanks."

Taking off my jeans would be the biggest problem. Peeling off wet jeans was like trying to escape from cement. I wasn't looking forward to it. As Terono returned to the paddleboard, Arctok waggled his eyebrows at me. "Need help taking all this off?"

"Nice try," I said, grinning. He was a bit of a flirt, and despite the differences between our species, despite the fact I had nearly been a human taco for a kraken, he made it easy to take it in stride. Arctok had that kind of goofy, flirty attitude I liked.

He grinned but whatever he was about to say was cut off by Kron's gruff voice. "Arctok. We need wood and some water, if we can find any."

"I'll get wood for the fire," Arctok said with a wink at me. "You can warm the bed for my return."

"In your dreams," I said, rolling my eyes.

"I don't know what that means, but I will take it as a promise."

Arctok smirked at my blush before entering the trees and disappearing. Leaving me with his friends—brothers? I swallowed as awkwardness crept over me. I didn't know these guys—aliens, I reminded myself. What if they saved me from the kraken just to cook me over the fire?

But they seemed innocent enough, Terono fiddling with the board's undercarriage while Kron set up what looked like a cooking spit with well-practiced movements. For a girl who thought of camping as a five star cabin with a jacuzzi, it was disturbing to see someone familiar with the outdoor life. But as another shiver wracked my body, I turned around to focus on putting on dry clothes.

Peeling myself out of wet clothes was as pleasant as traffic in Los Angeles. Gross and slightly traumatizing. I grimaced as my cold hoodie stuck to my chilled skin, throwing it and my shirt to the ground. My bra was more difficult—my arms and hands were still stiff from the cold and it was nearly impossible to unclasp it behind me.

"Terono," Kron snapped.

A glance over my shoulder showed them both pointedly turned away. My skin prickled. Relieved, I faced forward again and my fingers finally worked the clasp open. I dropped it on top of my discarded clothes and pulled on the shirt, which swamped me and hung down to my knees. At least I wasn't totally bare now and could use this to hide my ass while I took off my jeans.

Peeling off my jeans would be the hard part. I wasn't exactly a fan of loose, bootcut jeans. Give me jeans that molded to my ass like stickers on oranges. My ass was my biggest—ha!—and best attribute, so why not emphasize it? Now my big ass made this difficult. Crap.

"Are you... in pain?" came the tentative question behind me

after several minutes of me struggling to yank my jeans over my butt.

"Uh—um, no. Nope. Just... ugh, struggling to get these off – not meant to get, ugh, wet."

The next time he asked, he was a lot closer behind me. "Can I help somehow?"

The thought made my chilled skin heat. Totally out of embarrassment. Completely. Nothing to do with my imagination conjuring an image of an alien that looked better than ninety percent of the actors I ran across hooking his thumbs into my jeans. Ahem.

I smiled over my shoulder at Kron, playing with fire. "Ask me in about five minutes if I still can't get these damn things off."

"A female has her pride," he said with a nod, a gleam of amused understanding in his silver eyes making him relatable. And sinfully sexy, but I tried not to see that. I faced forward again, grinning. It was probably the hormones from nearly being a kraken snack, but I could enjoy a little flirtation.

"So, um, thank you again for rescuing me. It seemed like you had a beef with those guys."

"They stole from us," Kron said as he retreated. "Two days ago, they raided our compound. Others told us not to settle near the ocean, that they were insufferable neighbors, but we thought those Moxic were mild annoyances. They've done honest business with us before. But we were wrong. We planned their comeuppance today."

Terono, sounding distracted, added, "And we saw your stasis pod fall. We hoped to get to it first—the tech in those slaver ships isn't unique, but the salvage is good."

"Oh." So they hadn't come for *me* at all. A small tarnish on their hero status but after a moment I told myself to knock off the pity party. They *had* rescued me. My jeans went down an inch.

"So, what happened to you?"

"I, uh, don't know. I woke up when they took me out of my pod. They didn't exactly hurt me. But they talked about some great monster and danced around me for a bit before they made me drink this gross stuff that tasted like fish. Then they punted me out into the ocean." I breathed a sigh of relief as my jeans slipped the next few inches and over the widest part of my hips. All good from here. "My first foray into space travel has been a little *too* eventful."

"What ejected you from the slaver ship?"

"It was a slaver ship?" The tremble in my voice was real, too real. "What... what do they do with slaves?"

"Sell them, work them on ships, in compounds and whore-houses. Humans can fetch a hefty price, if I remember right."

"You do," Terono said.

My hands paused in their work. "Are you... do you plan—"

"Our people do not condone slaves," Kron said. "It is not done. We will bring you to the Hub where you can find passage off this planet. It is nowhere a lone female should be."

My relief made it easier to force my jeans down my legs. The shirt covered me as I bent and peeled the jeans from my calves. Freedom. Nothing better.

Except for having my own clothes, in my own cramped apartment. But I couldn't have everything.

"Do you think I can find someone to take me back to my home?"

"Maybe," he said.

"That didn't sound very confident."

"This planet deals with criminals and scum like us. I can only hope to get you *off* this planet. From there, I don't know."

My shoulders dropped, my jeans were finally free but I... I wasn't. Would I ever get home? Kron didn't seem optimistic about my chances, and the uncertainty of my position made a yawning gulf open inside me.

I strode to a nearby rock and stretched my clothes across it, using brisk movements to remind myself I couldn't do anything about the future. What was it that homeless yogi told me one day? Besides the amazing properties of cabbage? The greatest fear should be your present, not the future.

Okay, so he may've been crazy and not a yogi, but the guy lived on my apartment's stoop. I liked a good inspirational pep talk. The point was, I shouldn't worry about this now. Couldn't I just be amazed I was *literally speaking to aliens?*

I turned away from the rock to Kron, busy piling rocks around where the fire would be.

"Can I help any?" I asked. Anything to get my mind off how dire my situation was.

"Know how to use a knife?"

"I can chop things," I offered. "I'm an expert chopper."

He leaned back, watching me with amusement, showing off the broad muscles across his chest as he did so. "And skinning animals?"

"Er, not so much."

"Then open this and set up the beds," Kron said. "We'll want them close to the fire. You take the one in the middle. Enemies frequent these trees."

I blinked, looking around. "T-they do?"

"It's Reazus Prime. The only person you can trust is yourself."

Taking the pack from Kron, I opened it and started laying out what looked like sleeping bags. Now this at least seemed familiar. I knelt down, careful not to moon the guys as I prepped the area. "Not you guys?" I asked, keeping the conversation flowing. I wanted to know everything about this place and more importantly, the guys I would be camping with tonight.

"Not anyone, not here," Kron said.

"You, er, said that before, about this planet being not so awesome. Why?"

"It is a prison planet," said Terono, not looking up from the paddleboard. "Or was," he added as my heartbeat started to race in my ears. "It was abandoned some time ago."

"Except for those dancing weirdos and you guys."

Kron clucked his tongue. "And more. It's become a place for outcasts and criminals now, for those hiding from the reach of the authorities."

"And you're those kinds of people?" Maybe being saved wasn't such a good thing after all.

"We are criminals, yes," Kron said.

I grimaced and looked between them. "Please say you were unfairly charged and you're living here while you seek proof that you're innocent?"

Kron tilted his head, staring at me as if I had just grown bat wings. "Why would we say that?"

I turned back to the sleeping packs. Perfect. I was hanging out with criminals on an *outlaw* planet. At least they had the decency to rescue me from the kraken before they... did whatever to me. The trees were an inviting distance away. I could make a run for it.

And they would chase you down and clean their teeth with your knucklebones.

There. Two beds, both of them twice as long as I was. The right size for these three criminals I was making camp with deep inside this isolated forest on a planet I didn't know. I stretched out the third sleeping bag.

"I, uh, don't suppose you'll tell me why you're helping me?"

"We could always *not* help you."

"Terono," Kron snapped.

Terono clacked his teeth at the other alien, casting an irritated glance my way before he faced the paddleboard again. The innards of it were strewn all over the ground around him. "We need to go to the Hub for parts. We may as well take you, female. You wouldn't survive without us anyway."

"True enough," I said.

As much as it pained me to admit it, they were literally my

only allies here. Terono seemed satisfied by my answer and turned back to the electronics strewn on the ground around him.

I sat back on the newly unrolled sleeping bag. "If you guys hadn't shown up, I'd be dead."

Arctok strode out of the forest then with what looked like a large rat slung over his shoulder, a bundle of wood under his arm, and a devious grin on his face. He threw the bundle to the ground in front of Kron.

"Technically, you owe us your life, female, but we'll take your company for a few hours instead."

"Few hours?" Terono snorted. "That's optimistic."

"Food first, then discussion," Kron said with a wary glance at the sky. "It will grow dark soon. You, female—"

"I'm happy to help with whatever. And it's Natalie."

"Natalie." He softened a little and I got a funny feeling in my stomach from how he said my name. "Your duty is to sit close to the fire once my covey mate here lights it."

Arctok snorted. "And what are you going to be doing? I've hunted and gathered wood, Terono is working on our transport. What will you do besides take the attention of our pretty guest?"

"I will skin this puny gonc you've brought us. Hopefully there is at least enough for the—Natalie."

4

"We are weaponsmiths. The greatest in the star system. From tiny devices hidden as specks of dust to humongous planet destroyers. Destruction comes in many forms and our hands work the medium with skill and care. We grew rich with our efforts, and the whole system respected our covey. Our contracts included whole armies, and we equipped them with weapons only dreamed of before. And then..."

Terono had a lulling voice and if not for the topic at hand, if not for the fact we were eating space rat, the gonc, around a fire, I would have found myself searching for a pillow. I stared at him with wide eyes instead, the surprisingly good space rat forgotten in my hands.

"Then?" I prompted.

Kron snorted, drawing my attention. "We forgot the authorities can be fickle. What they give, they can also take."

Arctok turned to me. "The government happily bought our weapons. But then they required us to stop selling to others, claiming we were arming criminals and outlaws and warlords."

"Which is true enough. That *is* the business," Kron said.

Terono sat back on his hands. "The government didn't like

this. They said to give it up or they would shut us down and throw us onto the prison planet. And thus we ended up here."

"But I thought this wasn't a prison planet anymore."

"He's skipping the good parts: the fighting, the militia we formed in our name, the siege against a government outpost to get back a collection of our weapons they seized from a so-called terrorist." Arctok shrugged. "Reazus Prime was our only option after that. We do not have our former glory and riches, but we at least have our respect."

"We are no government pawn." Terono spat to the side and it went a surprisingly long distance.

"But don't they have a point? Isn't it, y'know, *bad* to sell weapons to warlords and criminals?"

"So the government should sell our weapons to those very same warlords?" Terono snorted when he saw my expression. "Yes, female, our government is not above profiting off those bad criminals. We were getting in their way of a monopoly."

"The governments back on Earth do shady things too," I said, vaguely recalling someone telling me about the police agencies losing drugs in monitored deals with cartels. Going into the ethics of the police selling guns and drugs seemed sketchy, and now so did judging these guys for not wanting to stop doing business. I had no idea what life was like in this world of theirs. Better to keep my trap shut than pretend I did.

But I did have one thing to say. "My name is Natalie. Not female."

Arctok barked a laugh as Terono glared at me over the fire. I shrugged and bit into the space rat. Good stuff. Like almost too spicy chicken. Space rat on a stick might be my new favorite meal.

"*Natalie,*" he said.

"*Terono,*" I said, stressing his name in the same way. His eyes narrowed before he huffed and turned back to fiddling with his tech. Kron caught my eye and smiled slightly.

"How long have you been away from Earth?" he asked.

The question sobered me.

"I'm not sure," I said, looking down. "I went to work—it was close to Christmas so I bundled up a little more. I remember that. What month is it here?"

"Month?" Kron shared a nonplussed look with Arctok.

"Nevermind," I sighed, looking down at my lap. "Time probably moves differently up here anyway. I just remember waking up on the spaceship with those green guys."

"The slavers," Arctok said. "I'm surprised we haven't run across any search parties."

"The ship was pretty destroyed. There might not be any left to search for her and her brethren."

Arctok's face darkened. "They could be in a mega blast and find a way to survive."

The green guys were the equivalent of space cockroaches then. Space cockroaches who liked to steal women from Earth. A thought niggled at me and I looked up. "Wait, so... more women could have escaped? Like me?"

"Those pods are not only designed to keep the inhabitant in stasis, but to evacuate in an emergency to the nearest planet surface," Kron explained. "There could very well be more females."

"Is there any way to find them?"

Terono didn't look up as he appeared to test a doodad on the electrical component he studied in his lap. Absently, he said, "There is no way to track a pod unless you have its signal in advance or can guess somehow. We knew of your pod because we saw its descent to the surface."

"If they are smart, they have hidden themselves or found a strong protector."

I bristled at the implication... until I remembered this wasn't Earth and my first interaction with aliens here ended up with me nearly becoming a toothpick cleaning a kraken's fangs. Right. My indignation burned into ash. Girl power was all well and good until you crash landed on a hostile alien planet. Then you needed allies.

"You said you would take me to the Hub in the morning," I said, turning to Kron. "What is that? Do you think I'll find humans there?"

"The Hub is the main landing stage for the planet. It is so-named because it was the hub where food deliveries used to arrive when this place was a prison. Now it is a larger community and ships arrive and depart continuously from there. If there is one place where we can negotiate for you to return home to Earth or get off the planet, it is there."

"You may find some of your people there too," Arctok said, his voice softer. "We will help you search in the morning."

Terono huffed and all eyes turned to him. What was his problem? Didn't he have a single ounce of sympathy in him? Terono threw down the part he had spent the last little while testing. With a massive irritated grunt, he said, "In the morning is a long shot. It looks like we'll be on foot."

"You couldn't get it working?"

"I thought the wiring was loose from the damn hits from that beast, but combined with the water the wires have eroded past usability." He rubbed his face, and his bone deep tiredness made me wince in sympathy. "What's sitting over there is a pile of junk now, barely fit for salvage."

Kron and Arctok both groaned.

"What does this mean?" I asked, throwing Terono a cautious glance.

He dropped his hand and blinked at me wearily. "It means you best ensure your shoes are dry, female."

Kron sighed, seeming just as gutted as Arctok. He gave me a wary glance before looking toward the sky as if searching for an answer.

"We will discuss this more in the morning. For now, rest and recuperate, Natalie. We may have a long journey ahead of us."

As if he'd given me permission, my body nudged me and drew my attention to all the aches and pains of the day. Tiredness tugged at my limbs and now with my belly full, the sleeping bags behind me looked as good as a feather bed.

I said goodnight and threw my stick and the leftover bones into the fire. The guys discussed setting up a watch while I crawled into the sleeping bag in the middle.

"There's little to no activity in the area, at least from anything bigger than a gonc," Arctok told the others.

"I'll set up a perimeter at least," Terono said. "Anything crosses it and they'll regret it."

"Set it up a little ways out to give us some warning."

"I know how to set up a perimeter, Kron."

"Of course. And you know how to drive the hovercraft in active combat."

There were some grunts and the sound of roughhousing. My eyes closed, a tiny smile on my lips. These guys weren't so bad. Neither was this sleeping bag. It seemed to have its own heating source, and my toes curled into the soft, heated fabric. Whatever heated it didn't extend all the way up, but at least the fire was there to keep my shoulder and arm warm as I turned onto my side, pillowing my head on my hand. I had expected to feel like I was sleeping on the ground, but it wasn't like that at all. My own bed at home wasn't this comfortable. All I missed was a pillow.

Sleep dragged me under then with the guys' voices providing lulling background noise. I didn't remember stasis, not actively. But something must have lingered in my subconscious because my dreams were misty, unclear, waves of light and the whoosh of something that sounded like a ventilator keeping me under.

Cold touched me. So very cold. I shuddered and my teeth chattered. It was so cold...

Vaguely, like I was outside myself, I felt my body curling in on itself, trying to preserve what little warmth remained.

"Cold, little one? Come here."

A sigh escaped me as warmth threaded its way around me. Waking a little, I found myself curled into someone's arms, my face pressed against a warm body. As I burrowed closer, nose pressed to his neck, my savior released a shaky breath.

"Arctok?"

His arm tugged me closer, hand curling over my backside in a way that made heat pulse at my center. I imagined it would be so much better if he had slipped his arm into the sleeping bag. "Mm, yes. Now sleep."

He was so very warm and combined with the sleeping bag, I was now comfortable. "Thanks."

"Having a soft female cuddled up to me? My pleasure."

Attraction and desire mingled lazily in my middle at his rumbling, rough voice. But sleep was there, holding me as close as he was, and I couldn't help but give in.

There were no dreams this time. Just warmth and pleasure, hazy and indistinct. Desire plucked at me like strings on a guitar, growing in size until my thighs were rubbing together.

My lashes fluttered open. Need twisted around me and so did Arctok, his body pressing mine down as he laid to the side of me, face buried against my neck. Heat crept up my spine, wet kisses trailing over my neck, his hot breath in my ear.

How had I ended up like this? And why was my hand—

Oh god. He was huge under my hand. Covered, but huge, the fabric stretched tightly over him. And I was stroking him through his pants, and I thought I might've been at it for a while with the wet spot forming on the fabric.

I started this, I realized. Somehow in my sleep, my horny self had gotten the better of me and now I was giving an alien an over-the-pants handy. And now Arctok's hand slid over the silky sleeping bag and created the most delicious friction against my hard nipples. He groaned a little as my breath stuttered.

He was no angel, but neither was I, and his rough touch

made me tremble. This was so wrong, so weird, but in the dark with his needy breaths in my ear, nothing seemed better than arching into his touch. Arctok turned his head, sliding teeth against my skin, and my head turned toward his, the meeting of our lips inevitable.

He kissed like a drug, soaking into my system in moments and driving the pleasure centers of my mind wild. Addiction would be easy with his teasing nips and the deep curl of his tongue as he pulled my taste from me. I held him to me with my free hand, wanting more, knowing there would be no recovering from this.

There was no tempering my need. No beating back the rising tide surging up the banks as he slipped his hand under the sleeping bag and made the waves pulse. Plucking at my nipples through my shirt, tracing the curves of my body, squeezing my asscheek.

His hips thrust his cock into my hand and I imagined crazy things. Rolling over and letting him slide that monstrous thing into me. Climbing on top of him and seeing how far I could take him in my mouth. Fucking him until sweat slicked our skin. When his hand slipped between my thighs, the sweetest joy burst on my tongue, my moan swallowed by him.

His hand was confident, sure. Gathering up my slick pleasure and swirling it back into my skin. My hips arched for him and he responded, not letting me suffer for a moment, my clit aching under his insistent touch.

"Natalie," he groaned, breathing my name against my lips. He drew away, dropping quick kisses down my chin and neck as he angled himself down. My hand fell back, his cock slipping out of my grip as he moved down my body. The sleeping bag rustled as he moved it down, dipping his head to capture my nipple in his mouth.

"Yes," I hissed, letting my head drop.

So wrong... but at least aliens knew how to do it right.

He scraped his teeth against me before sucking, wet fabric

sticking to me as he rolled his tongue around the tender nub. My fingers were numbing, fizzles of pleasure climbing under my skin as he moved to the other one, tending to it with the same dedicated care. His fingers and mouth played me expertly, causing pulses of need to climb and climb, making my legs fall apart for his thick fingers as he fucked me with them, his thumb pressing my clit. A poor imitation of his huge cock, but something to fill the ache within me.

Stars always fascinated me. But in the city the light pollution made it impossible to see them. When my eyes opened wide, pleasure spiking and the fever of orgasm shaking through me, it was fascinating to see them shining up above, see them witnessing Arctok fucking me with his fingers, see me needy and whining under his touch. Darkness shed away and all that was left was light, shining and white gold, expanding across my vision until it burned away everything else.

"That's it, that's what I want," Arctok murmured. My vision returned in time to see him leaning back to watch, the cold sweeping in to kiss at my wet nipples. I shook around him and satisfaction tightened his face.

I reached for him, nails digging into his shoulders. He came willingly, his mouth hot, an amused hum in the back of his throat.

"Again?" he asked.

I laughed, breathless and quiet. Out of the darkness came a rustle and I stiffened.

Oh god. Kron and Terono must've heard all that. The sleeping bags weren't far apart at all. If I reached out, I could touch the one on my other side. That meant they had heard everything and there was no doubt about what we were doing.

"None of that," Arctok murmured, leaning down and capturing my mouth again. "They don't mind waking up to such splendor."

Embarrassment and, strangely, aching desire washed over me. They didn't mind? He knew that? Did that mean...? I gasped into his mouth with the implications, imagining them both sitting in their sleeping bags with hard-ons.

Arctok kept the fire stoked between my legs, luring out the last pulses of my orgasm with gentle swirls of his finger. He regained my attention by the simple expedient of tugging my bottom lip between his teeth.

He pulled back. "Can I share this with my covey mates?"

"What do you mean?" I murmured.

"Your pleasure," Arctok rumbled, nipping at my ear. His fingers swirled below, gathering up more of my slickness he'd inspired. "Let me share this with them."

"I, um..."

"Just a taste," he promised. "To whet the appetite."

When he said it like that... my thighs clenched against his hand. "Okay."

The noise he made, pleased and viciously satisfied, made the hair on my arms stand up. He lifted, withdrawing his hand carefully. I turned my head to the side as he sat up and followed his gaze to where Kron was propped up on his side beside us. I swallowed. There was enough light from the stars and moon to see the gleam in his eyes.

Arctok extended his hand to him. He held my gaze as he grabbed Arctok's wrist and wrapped his mouth around one of his glistening digits. I held my breath as he pulled back, that stare of his hot enough to burn through my sleeping bag.

If I wasn't already wet, just staring into his eyes right then was enough to soak through panties. My chest was tight. Los Angeles could be wild... but I had never experienced something as wild as this. Something I wanted like this.

Then Arctok turned. Reluctance to pull away from Kron's gaze made me too late to watch what Terono did, but I heard the result. A groan, needy and harshly cut off, tugged at my middle. Knowing the tech-obsessed alien made that noise because of *me* was a power I didn't need.

"There," Arctok said, returning to me. He stretched himself

out on his side next to my body and tugged up the sleeping bag to my shoulders. Rumpled and feeling well spent, I curled against him, slipping my arm out so I touched his warm chest. He was still insistently hard against my leg. When I drew my hand down, he trapped my hand in his.

"Sleep," came Kron's soft voice. "There's time for that later."

"Hopefully soon," Arctok said, nudging my hair away with his nose.

A rustle behind me and heat pressed against my back. I held my breath as Kron curled his arm over my waist, tucking me neatly against his chest. "Sleep," he said, ruffling my hair. His tone didn't have room for argument.

I closed my eyes and found it surprisingly easy to slip back to sleep between them.

5

"I think I can go do my business without someone following me."

"Really?" Kron asked, licking the last of whatever fruit he'd brought back for breakfast off his thumb. We were the first ones up and Arctok and Terono were big lumps on the ground surrounded by morning dew. "And if there are enemies in the trees? What will you do to protect yourself?"

God, my bladder was about to kill me. I gave a harassed, hopeless glance toward the trees. "I'll think of something."

"When I asked if you were good with a knife, you said you were an excellent chopper. Forgive me if I remain skeptical of your combat skills." He smirked at my scowl and turned back to the fire. "Take Arctok. He'll give you privacy."

I opened my mouth, intending to remind him Arctok was asleep when Arctok said, "Come on, little one." I spun and found him standing up, hand held out and head cocked. He looked attractively rumpled despite his lack of a shirt and, despite the scar across his face, he had a boyish charm to him. A teasing smirk played on his mouth as he looked down at me.

I flushed, still only wearing the too-big shirt. My clothes were still damp and Kron had relit the fire to help them dry off further before we left. Mist clung to my ankles but the rest of me was very much exposed, my hard nipples obvious under the thin fabric.

"I found a stream yesterday," Arctok said. "I'll need to collect water for us anyway."

My bladder made itself known again and I grunted. "Fine, fine, let's just hurry."

Arctok gestured me ahead and huffed in amusement as I stormed past him into the trees. Sticks and brush poked my bare feet, but the insistent urge in my middle required relief and I didn't have time to waste.

"Up ahead and to the right is a copse of bushes," Arctok called after me. I spared him a thankful wave and hurried onward. His footsteps stopped as I found the bushes and squatted down behind them. Blessed relief followed.

Look at me, Dad, peeing in the bushes. And he said I'd never be brave enough to rough it.

I searched for something to wipe with. Poison oak was a real thing, right? What was the space equivalent? Caution made me refrain from grabbing one of the large leaves off the bush and I drip dried for a good minute before standing up, my knees popping from squatting for so long.

"Feel better?" Arctok asked when I came back into view.

"Much," I said, wiping off a stray leaf that was stuck to the front of my comically large shirt. I clapped my hands together. "Where to next, boss?"

He nodded forward. "The river is not too far this way. Are your feet okay without protection?"

"I'll step carefully," I promised him. "I can carry one of those."

He had grabbed two canteens on the way out of camp and he handed one over to me without complaint. It was surprisingly light and made out of some silvery metal I didn't recognize. He forged forward, heavy boots making the path easier for me if I stayed in his footsteps. I admired his back, the sheer muscle on display in his huge shoulders. If not for the inhuman coloring of his skin—or his size—I might've been looking at the back of one of the bodybuilders who liked to hang out by the boardwalk. Except this one didn't have the acrid smell of bulking powders lingering around him.

He glanced over his shoulder at me. "How did you sleep?"

I bit the inside of my lip, hiding my smile. "*Fine*. How about you?"

"Could've been better if someone had shared their sleeping bag."

I laughed and saw the hint of his grin as he slowed to walk beside me. "You should've asked one of your friends. Or wait. Are they your brothers?"

If so, that scene last night turned from erotic to weird in a heartbeat.

He made a face. "Brothers? Ack! No, a covey cannot exist with members of your blood."

"Why not?" I asked, though relief spilled through me.

"Because when we take a mate or mates, the connection is shared between all of us." Arctok shuddered theatrically, making me laugh again. "I do *not* wish to know what my brothers think and feel while mating."

I looked forward, chewing on the inside of my lip as memories from the night before came back. How Kron looked at me... Terono's ragged groan, cutoff as if trying not to embarrass himself. "So you're saying... when we, er, last night..."

"When you took your pleasure like a goddess from me," Arctok said and my head jerked up. His gaze swept over me as if he wouldn't mind a repeat. I flushed and it wasn't wholly desire, but greedy vanity too. Goddess. I'd never been compared to a goddess before.

"Er, yes." I coughed to clear my embarrassment away. It didn't work. Arctok grinned and I faced forward. "That. So they felt that? Through this connection?"

We reached the stream, a tiny thing with what looked like

too many sticks and rocks in it to be really useful. I pushed the question to the back of my mind as Arctok pointed me to a spot where the stream widened. I knelt down beside him, careful not to get my shirt wet, and we filled our canteens, our arms brushing.

Arctok sat his canteen aside when it was full and bent over the stream, splashing his face with water and scrubbing it. It looked so refreshing and cold, I bent next to him and splashed my face too. It was cold enough to turn the tips of my fingers red, but worth it for how refreshed I felt when I sat up.

Arctok stared at me when I looked up, and my gaze followed a drop of water running down his jaw. His gaze held memories and promise.

"My covey mates could feel and hear everything last night. Every moment."

My blush burned away the last of the cold water lingering on my cheeks. Arctok chuckled and reached out, fingertips grazing my jaw before sliding down to my neck. His heavy-lidded silver eyes were easy to fall into.

"Every moment," he repeated in a rasp that went right to my core. The hairs on my arms rose as his hand moved down my arm, thumb so, so close to brushing my breast. His eyes dropped to my lips as they parted. "Though I daresay they would have much rather it be *them* between your legs, tasting you from the source. Which reminds me that *I* did not get a proper taste at all."

My voice was strangled. "That's your fault."

A devious grin spread over his features. "So it is. I'll remediate it promptly."

I braced myself, forgetting our surroundings with Arctok's heady touch.

"Arctok!"

The shout came through the forest. I jumped, head whipping toward the noise.

Arctok groaned, a chest-deep sound of frustration that

made a purely feminine trill ring through my body. Then he pinned me with those inhuman but very sexy eyes. "Pause this. We'll resume at another time."

"Right." I swallowed. Don't overthink this, Nat. I pushed myself to my feet, avoiding his eyes, nervous and giddy as a schoolgirl flirting with a guy in front of the water fountain.

Crazy, right? He was an alien. His covey mates, whatever that was, *could hear and see me* when we mated.

Yet he was the hottest man—alien—I'd ever seen.

On edge and wishing I had panties, I followed Arctok back to the campsite. Terono was up now and he and Kron glanced our way as we arrived. The suns had scared the mist away a little. I went to my clothes which someone had hung up on sticks close to the fire. Dry enough to put on now. The guys all made themselves busy, backs facing me, when I took my clothes a little ways away and changed.

My socks and shoes were, thankfully, completely dry.

Kron was talking when I came back and he helpfully included me as he continued. "I was just explaining that it shouldn't take more than a few days to get to the Hub on foot. We'll find a guide or a ship for you to get out of here on."

"How's your leg?" Arctok asked as he handed me the bowl of berries we were having for breakfast.

"It feels fine. These are *really* good," I said after one of the purple berries burst on my tongue. It tasted like strawberry pear with the perfect amount of sourness to make you appreciate the sweetness. I wasn't much of a baker, but I could see myself making a ton of pies with these. Some sweet cream or, better, ice cream... Mmm...

I opened my eyes, realizing I had closed them with my vivid food dreams, and found Terono staring at me, electronic parts in front of him forgotten.

"Ahem." I grabbed another handful of berries and tried to hand the rest to him.

He shook his head, looking down. "I've had my share."

"We all have," Arctok said around the last of his. "Fill up."

Kron scratched out a crude map on the ground in front of him, using twigs and leaves to mark areas. "This is where we are. This is where we need to be." He pointed to where he'd dropped some kind of nut a good distance from the X marking our location.

"Not too bad," Arctok said.

Kron continued, pointing out our route with a stick. "We'll travel now and in the mornings and rest during the high point of the sun when it's hottest. How is your night vision?"

"Nonexistent. Sorry."

They didn't seem to mind, though I half expected Terono at least to be irritated by my limitations. "Then we'll travel in the evenings as long as we can," Kron said. "Everyone in agreement? Good. Let's pack. Terono, anything we can salvage?"

"I've set aside a few things. The core for one and some other bits. The rest of this is useless."

"You found a good hiding spot for them?"

"Marked it with stones and mud," he said.

"You're leaving the parts you want here?" I asked, following their conversation from my spot folding up the sleeping bags.

"We don't need it bogging us down," Terono said as he pushed off the ground. "It'll be easy to come back for them when we get a transport. And it's not as if it would be worth much in a trade if we happen to come across anyone. We're better off trading the sword."

"Hopefully it doesn't come to that," Kron said. "I'd rather spend credits on the Hub than sell the sword."

Terono didn't seem to mind. He picked up the sword where it stood against a tree. The size of it surprised me again. Terono didn't even look strained as he picked up a sword that looked as heavy as a fridge. He saw me gaping and a smirk curled his lips. I quickly looked away.

"It's no problem to make another," he said, and I felt his stare on my back as I finished packing up.

A cry cut through the forest. The bag fell out of my hands as the three aliens went on alert around me. Close. Whatever it was was close and coming fast, a rising chatter reaching us from the trees. A chatter my frozen body recognized.

Arctok spun to Terono who was closest. "Get her out of here!"

Terono threw him the sword which Arctok caught in both hands.

"It's going to be tough with just the two of us," he said as he turned to Kron.

"I know," Kron snarled. A spear embedded itself into the ground by his feet. Another one broke off against a tree behind Terono. "Go!" he said to us.

Terono clamped down on my arm and tugged me back. I had an instant before Terono dragged me away to see Kron and Arctok clasp forearms and bend their foreheads toward one another with fierce concentration in their expressions. Something changed around them, the air turning hazy and the surroundings indistinct. Then I was dragged away and needed to focus on running.

I didn't want to go, but being sacrificed to a fish wasn't on my bucket list. My heart pounded as we ran, Terono holding himself back to stick behind me, his body shielding mine from anything coming from our backs. Blood rushed in my ears, almost overwhelming the cry of the fighters meeting behind us in the clearing. Tree roots and brush tried to trip me up and I felt as ungainly as a toddler.

"Strike this!" Terono exclaimed when I stumbled over a rock I hadn't noticed.

The next instant, his arms grabbed me up. My breath left me as he tucked me into his chest and ran, the sound of the cultists following us through the trees.

6

"They're throwing spears!"

"I can see that!" Terono shouted. A spear thudded into the tree beside us at the same height as his head.

There must have been dozens of chattering aliens in the brush around us. Tracking our every move. Spears landed frighteningly close, the thuds like coconuts dropping to the sand. They would crack our heads like eggs if any hit us. Even with the rush of leaves as loud as a waterfall in my ears, I heard them closing in.

Our only option was to run. I hated it but there wasn't anything I could do but hold on. Terono's big frame wasn't built for running. Unlike the cultists who were lithe and limber, Terono was made for brute force smashing.

A howl echoed through the forest. "She has drunk the sacred oil! She is ours!"

"Strike that," hissed Terono, seemingly kicking up more speed.

"Eat trash!" I yelled over his shoulder.

He jumped over fallen logs, skidded down little gullies, sliding on leaves rotting on the ground. His grip nearly squeezed all the air out of me, but I would've been breathless anyway. The cries of the cultists ran down my spine like nails on a chalkboard. They would have me, it seemed to say, and I would *pay*.

But it seemed only seconds after the chilling thought, the noise of our pursuers stuttered out. Over Terono's shoulder, the trees moved with the wind, not with any sort of furious pursuit.

"I think they're gone." I raised my voice to be heard over his loud, huffing breaths. "Hold up, I think they fell back."

Like a car needing a moment to fight momentum and brake, it took a few seconds for Terono to slow, but he did, blowing out a breath as he finally stopped. He turned, facing the direction we'd come from.

The forest remained silent.

"Shouldn't we hear the guys?"

"Not necessarily," he said. It took a moment for me to understand his meaning. When I did, I tightened my hands on his shoulders. We wouldn't hear Arctok and Kron if they were dead.

He darted a look at me and huffed.

"Not dead, princess. Our bond would not hide that from me. They are out there stalking the last of their prey."

"Oh. I forgot about that." The bond let them hear and feel each other. Terono would definitely know if they were dead. "Can you tell where they are?"

Terono half-closed his eyes. "Not far. Coming this way."

"Good."

"They killed many," Terono said with a smug curl of his lips.

"Er... great."

"Remember they would gladly sacrifice you to their monstrous underwater god."

"I know," I whispered.

"So you should feel victorious that your champions have beat them back."

"Right." His lips turned down at my one word answers and

I hurriedly said, "Why are you talking like we're in a Renaissance Faire? Princess and champions and whatnot?"

"A what?" He shook his head. "I'm not speaking in any kind of way. If you find the way I speak distasteful, we'll stand here in utter silence."

"No!" I yelped, as he started to drop me to the ground. Being on the ground when those cultists might be out there... Grimacing, I shot him an abashed look and clung to his shoulders. "Sorry. I thought you were making fun of me. Don't drop me."

Calling me princess because I couldn't deign to run on my own. A useless human who couldn't keep my legs under me. Without them, I'd be toast and there was no denying it.

Terono's quiet voice had the soothing effect of a mother's hand on my temple. "I would not."

My stomach squirmed in response. I could totally be the princess if he wanted to play the knight. My teeth dug into my lower lip. Dangerous. I was treading on shaky ground with this desire for these aliens. This wasn't my world. These weren't my people. We might not even have sex the same way! And what about protection and birth control? There was no way I'd return to Earth knocked up with an alien baby.

But at the same time, pressed up against Terono's chest, my thoughts were decidedly non-platonic.

The sound of people approaching distracted me and I turned my head toward the source right as Arctok and Kron came out of the trees. They must have known through their bond that I was safe and sound, but the flash of relief in Arctok's eyes when he saw me made my stomach clench. He returned my smile with one that was heart-stopping with its sexiness.

Kron lugged the huge sword over his shoulder, following Arctok up the side of the hill toward them. "*That* is why I don't want to sell the sword."

"I think you're right. It is far too useful. Anyway, the

chances of coming across a traveling band seems slim with them"—Arctok jerked a finger over his shoulder to the forest —"skulking about."

Terono let me down and I slid gracelessly to my feet. "They're still out there?" I asked, brushing off the leaves on my jeans.

"They slunk off when they realized they had too many casualties."

"You think they'll go back to their pit and stay there?" Terono asked.

"Probably not," Kron said, wiping at something on his face I hoped was dirt. "So let's drive on. It's a long journey ahead of us."

Chewing the inside of my lip, I looked at the three aliens and took in the dirt and blood smeared on their faces, the exhaustion in their faces. This wasn't fair to them.

"Look... how long would it take you to get home?"

Arctok narrowed his eyes. "Why do you ask?"

Leaves rustled as I shifted nervously under his heavy gaze. Somewhere close by, a creature's claws scrabbled on tree bark as it ran into the thick canopy. "You've done so much for me without knowing me. Are you sure you want to keep going?"

Terono snorted. "Can you survive by yourself?"

Probably not, but I lifted my chin and took a deep breath. "I don't need to drag you guys into this."

Terono shared a smirk with the other aliens before placing his hand on my shoulder. "Come, princess. Like Kron said, it's a long journey."

Arctok grinned at me as I huffed. "Fine. You go on ahead, if you wish. We'll just walk in the same direction."

The guys chuckled as I rolled my eyes. Real jokesters. I turned on my heel, and started forging a path ahead, slapping away the branches tearing at my sleeves.

"Glorious leader, do you know which direction is the Hub?"

I gritted my teeth and slowed to a stop. "No," I muttered.

"What was that?" Trampling the brush underfoot Arctok reached me and put his hand to his ear. "My gentle ears could not hear you. Ah! You wound me." He rubbed his side where I'd dug the sharp point of my elbow.

"Don't tease her," Kron said as he and Terono fell into step behind us, the both of them snickering together. "She is our honorable charge. Or perhaps a tiny mascot."

"Har har. Maybe I should've taken the kraken over these tired jokes."

I caught Arctok's eye and blushed as he winked.

"We can tire you out in other ways, if you wish."

7

We walked. All day.

They weren't kidding about us needing to break at the hottest point of the day. We left the forest by midday, stepping into a vast plain with tall grasses and the occasional massive tree spreading its shade over the land. There were wind-worn rock formations, the haze of a mountain in the distance. We walked toward the mountain and stopped in the shade under one of these giant trees. The heat made us uncomfortable and we kept our conversation short and to the point as we rested or otherwise tried to escape the heat.

Terono spread himself out at the base of the tree in the grass, throwing his arm over his face. I stretched out a short distance away from Arctok and Kron, debating if it would be bad manners to strip down to my underwear. It was worse than any LA heatwave.

"Do we *have* to have a fire?" Terono groaned an hour later as the first licks of flame in our shady area turned the barely bearable heat on its head. I turned toward them, wrinkling my nose at the extra heat as it reached me.

"Only if you can eat raw meat," Kron snapped back. He wiped the sweat off his brow and leaned back from the orange flames reaching for the sky. "Since you have the energy to complain, you can go catch dinner."

"In this heat?" Terono huffed and stretched his legs out, a *no way in Hell* if I ever saw one.

Tired of even watching the two, I looked back to the great canopy overhead. Crumpled grass underneath my back poked at me. Light danced through the holes between the leaves and somewhere nearby, an insect buzzed. My eyelashes grew heavy with more sleep.

A cold nose touched my arm.

I jerked and the little creature startled, jumping back a couple paces. But it didn't go far, its pointed nose twitching at me and beady eyes assessing me warily. For a critter that was a mix of an arctic fox and a mole, it was surprisingly expressive.

"Oh!" I exclaimed and offered my hand out to it. It cautiously sniffed my palm to decide if I was trustworthy. Finally, it did, and it leaned its long face into my hand. My heart instantly melted. "You're a cute thing, aren't you?"

"What's that, princess?"

Female. Princess. I rolled my eyes. When would Terono learn how to say my name?

"This little thing just came up to me and wanted to be petted. Just like a puppy!" I crooned with delight as the creature purred and wiggled onto my chest. So soft! It had fur like a long-haired kitten.

"It's a hawni."

Kron's tone made me stop scratching behind the creature's ears. I glanced over at them and my mouth went dry. "Oh god. Uh oh. It's dangerous. It's venomous, right? It's going to burrow into my chest and kill me, isn't it?"

Kron shared a look with Arctok who was staring with his lips parted. "Where do you get these things?"

"Uh, every space movie ever," I said.

Arctok shook his head and stood, holding his hand out as if

to calm the wild horse in front of him. Or the dangerous arctic fox/mole creature currently purring on my chest.

"Be very still," he said, his feet barely making a noise on the grass as he approached with slow, creeping strides.

He reached me and in one quick swoop, grabbed the hawni and snapped its neck.

As my shriek faded from the air, Arctok looked down at me, the hawni hanging limply from his hand. "Do you think you can get more?"

"M-more?" I gawked at the dead animal. "Why do you want *more*?"

He returned to the fire. "It's good meat," he said as Terono and Kron snickered. "Don't worry, they're an invasive species. You get ten credits per tail you bring to the Hub. Collect enough and you can pay for your own ride out of here." Terono snorted at my horrified face.

My head thudded against the hard ground and I squinted at the tree branches above head. I wasn't bothered by the heinous murder of a cute animal who came up to me for snuggles. It was a eat or be eaten world. It was sad, but we needed food.

My lip trembled. Poor thing.

There was a sniffling in the grass by my elbow. I turned my head and caught the small, beady eyes of another hawni. Probably looking for its friend, poor thing. It sat on its haunches and flicked its ears at me, tiny claws rubbing together.

"Uh, guys?" I called.

We had a good dinner that night when we stopped. I had collected, with their help doing the dirty deed, five tails.

Hey, when in Rome. Or conversely, when on Reazus Prime.

"Next we'll teach you how to skin them," Kron told me as

we sat near a different fire under a different tree. It was nearly sunset by the time we reached this spot close to the mountains. On the other side we would find the Hub waiting for us. A spring flowed through the rockface and we had managed to set up our camp nearby, the gentle sound of it burbling as good as any noise machine back home.

I grimaced as I laid back on the sleeping bag. With the coming night, the air turned chilly and I turned toward the fire's warmth. "I think I'll leave that in your capable hands, boss."

"Travelers."

That one word from Terono made all three of us sit up. I followed their gazes and found a slow caravan of vehicles moving out of the mountain path we planned to take in the morning, led by large horse-like creatures with tired, wrinkly faces and elephant skin.

"Stay close to us," Kron said as the three stood. I pushed myself up and hurried over to them, feeling like a nervous kid hiding behind my mom's legs again. Arctok put his hand on my back as I lingered near him, biting my lip and staring around Kron's back to the caravan as it came closer.

"They're coming from the Hub?" I asked, looking up to Arctok's tight face.

Kron answered. "They would be, yes. It's a band of Duviis. They're common around these parts, constantly traveling with no set home. We can expect good trade from them."

"With the clothes on our backs and a sword worth more than their entire caravan," Terono said with a snort. He returned to the fire. "We shouldn't even bother them with our poor offering."

"You sit and pout then," Kron said with good humor. Terono huffed and stretched out his legs, taking all the warmth we had abandoned.

The caravan closed in on us and stopped. There were five vehicles in all, rusted metal carts shaped like a big work-boot, with a windowed opening at the front for the driver to sit. Nearly noiseless except for the huffs and blurts of the horse-like elephants pulling them, I clearly imagined their caravan ceaselessly traveling the planet without disturbing any of the surroundings. They were the RV caravans of Earth.

"Greetings, weaponsmith."

The driver of the first metal boot disappeared from the window and I jumped as a new window slid open on the side of the cart. Like a food truck operator, he leaned out over the side and waved us toward him. "You've found our stock in healthy spirits, weaponsmith. Come see and be amazed."

"We thank you," Kron said formally as the three of us moved forward. Up close, the alien looked like an ancestor of one of the creatures driving his cart, his face wrinkled and his long snout turning toward us. The only thing separating him from his animal was his brilliant blue eyes which met mine and widened.

Arctok bristled and made a show of putting his hand on my shoulder. The alien's blue gaze flicked between him and Kron as if he couldn't believe what he was seeing. Kron and Arctok stared back and their magnificent size and uncanny eyes made the driver dip his head.

Kron relented at this show. "I'm afraid we have little to trade. Mainly hawni tails," he said with a question in his gaze as he deferred to me. I nodded, happy to be useful for once. "We will take some soap if you have it, and some water tablets in exchange for one of these tails."

The Duvii had a little smile playing around his mouth. "No weapons to trade, weaponsmith?"

"Unfortunately, no." When the driver looked toward the sword lazily propped up against the tree, Kron shrugged. "We have enough for us and no more."

"Ah, a pity. For once, I could trade for one of your mythical weapons."

"Hail us at our compound when you next travel near and we will happily trade with you."

The Duvii dipped his head to him. "Blessings upon you." His gaze flicked to me as I tried to figure out what was floating in all the jars at his back. "If you desire to trade the female..."

"Not happening," Arctok snapped, his hand clamping down on my shoulder.

The Duvii paled and raised his hands. "Understood, weaponsmith. I only seek to take the burden off your hands. The Hub is no good for trading the likes of her right now."

Arctok made a noise but Kron stepped in before he did more than bristle. "Thank you, but no. The female is not for sale. We seek only soap and some water tablets."

The Duvii happily took one of the animal tails in exchange for a medium bottle. "You may have this soap gratis," he said, handing over a brick of soap. He said goodbye and the caravan was off on its way again within minutes.

"In exchange for not cutting his head off," Arctok muttered with a sour look after them.

"My hero," I said, nudging him and receiving a begrudging smile in return.

Kron hefted the soap in his hands, a solid weight for such a small thing. "I'm going to wash off before nightfall. Natalie?"

"Hm?"

"Coming? Or do you wish to sleep in all the grime of the day?"

"Oh, um, coming."

Arctok smiled at my nervous glance at him. "I'll be manning the fire, I guess."

"And watching the view, you perverted *greck*," Terono called.

Arctok huffed as he sat down by the fire. "Take that back or I'll tell your mother when I next climb in her bed."

With their boisterous ribbing following us, we went to the

edge of the widest part of the stream. Kron sat down and pulled off his huge boots while I moved a little ways away, tugging off my hoodie.

"Why so far away? Surely you're not embarrassed to be nude in front of us."

I dropped my arms and threw my hoodie up the bank so it didn't get wet. "Maybe I'm trying to save you from the fish stink I have all over me."

Kron chuckled. "That's what the soap is for."

I didn't even have to lift my shirt to my nose to smell the combined mess of fish guts and sweat clinging to me. "Think we have time for my clothes to dry if I wash them?"

"Probably." Kron lifted his voice. "Terono, get off your ass and bring Natalie the spare shirt."

"Three of you and one spare shirt," I said, grinning as Terono's muttering complaints reached us. I toed off my shoes and socks.

"We travel light," Kron said, watching me unbutton my jeans. He saw me watching him and with a smirk, unbuckled his belt. "We didn't expect this human we found to require so many clothes. What is all this, by the way? Do you always cover your skin from neck to ankle?"

"Do you always keep a spare shirt when you don't even wear one?"

The buckle free, he pushed down his shorts and I got a good look at the package he smuggled as it flopped—*flopped* down near his knee. Jesus. His smirk grew as my eyes nearly popped out of my skull. "Wear a shirt? When it's your sole entertainment? We wouldn't dare do such a thing."

Too late, my eyes dropped to the ground, my face on fire. The old joke about the third leg came back. How much lube did these guys go through a year?

"You've-" I had to stop, clear my throat. "You've definitely made a spectacle of yourself," I said, striving for nonchalant, like I saw huge alien cocks all the time, and behind me Terono huffed a laugh.

He caught my eye from the bank as I looked over my shoulder. "Time for that entertainment to go both ways, princess."

I narrowed my eyes. Unlike Kron and Arctok, calmer and generally more thoughtful toward me, Terono constantly challenged. I thought he didn't like me at first. Now I knew it was his personality, sniping and rude but with a hot streak of compassion running through him.

None of that was in his expression now. Challenge rose there and mine rose to meet it.

Cheeks burning and adrenaline high, I whipped off my shirt. He caught it when it smacked against his chest and they barked out a laugh that echoed into the plains behind us. Terono's face split with a wide grin.

"There we go," he said. With jerky moves, I unsnapped my bra and let it fall to the ground. I didn't meet their eyes as I bent and shoved down my jeans, something wriggling inside my chest yelling at me to stop, they were laughing at me, I was some weird human with all the wrong parts and the wrong figure and why the *hell* had I started this?

I threw my jeans and underwear to the side and snapped my hand out to Kron. "Well?"

There was a pause. "The soap, you *greck*," Terono said with a snicker.

My gaze jumped up. Kron blinked a few more times, blatantly staring at me as if he'd bought tickets, before looking down around his feet for the soap. I bit the inside of my lip and glanced over my shoulder.

Terono's grin fell, replaced with a slow look that left me burning. "Don't play coy unless you plan to make good on it, princess."

8

"Soap."

Kron smacked it into my hand and I moved to stand in the stream, ice cold water hitting my shins reminding me not to get too comfy here. No sexing up the locals. Earth. Earth was the goal.

At the same time, what was the harm—besides walking funny in the morning?

As I bent down to dip the soap and lathered it, I wasn't immune to how their gazes lingered on my bare body. Los Angeles was a waterfall of a wild party and I had dipped my toes into the waters on occasion. But three? That stretched—ha ha—even my tolerance.

I washed quickly, self-conscious in the extreme as I washed between my legs and under my arms, rinsing off the dirt and grime of days. I tried not to think how I might need another bath a few hours from now.

I scoffed quietly. A few hours? Wasn't I optimistic?

The question at the forefront of my mind was one of regret. Looking back on this moment, would I wish I had dove in?

"Need some help back here?"

Kron's heat engulfed me as he stepped up to my back. My

stomach clenched, gaze darting up the bank to where Terono watched with lips parted. Fuck or flight time.

I tilted my head, drawing my hair over one shoulder. "Please," I murmured, handing him the soap. He took it, wrist brushing my shoulder, and my skin prickled under even that innocent touch.

Or maybe not so innocent. He trailed a finger down my spine, over every ridge, his breath grazing my bare skin.

"Sure you won't break?" he murmured and my nipples tingled.

I released a shaky breath. "No."

He passed the soap over my shoulders, the larger smelling like pine and a hint of mint that tickled my nose. It was antiseptic, making my skin tingle as he rubbed it down my shoulder blades, over my back, the dimples above my ass. I held onto my hair, keeping it out of the way as he dipped into every curve, patient and thorough in a way that made my heartbeat thrum in my ears.

It was almost a relief when his hand curved over my ass. Lathering me up and taking his sweet time about it, each swipe of his hand fueling the slickness between my thighs.

"I've been waiting to sink my teeth just... here," he said, and I heard the grin in his voice as he gripped my asscheek hard, making me moan.

My voice was tight. "Might want to wait until I rinse off."

He chuckled. "I can wait, but not too long. Them, however..." My gaze lifted to see Terono and Arctok staring at me from the bank, hungrily taking in my nude body, my pink nipples pebbling in the air, my flushed chest. "I can't promise they'll wait."

Kron's voice made me shiver. I couldn't promise I'd wait either. Only his erection grazing my ass reminded me of the dangers of this.

"So, am I the only one soaping up or what?"

Arctok was the first one to start down the bank, hand going to the buckle of his belt while his eyes held mine captive.

Terono followed with a sly grin. "Eyes to yourself, princess," he said as I unabashedly stared at Arctok as his shorts hit the ground. Water splashed as Arctok waded in toward us. He reached me and stopped, a hair's breadth away, my nipples brushing against his chest. "Care to spare some soap?"

Kron broke off a piece of the block and handed it over. "You scoundrels can share."

Arctok took it and handed it behind him, still staring at me like a snack cake after a twenty-four hour fast. I tortured my teeth under my lip as he languidly clasped my arms in his huge hands and let his fingers trace down my elbows and over my forearms until he loosely gripped my wrists.

"You don't have to do this."

I tilted my head back to meet his silver gaze. "No, I don't."

He wet his bottom lip and my attention dropped to the movement, the intensity of it all rising as we reached the inter-section between revving the engine and hitting the interstate or turning back to park in the safety of the garage.

I wanted the interstate.

Arctok's eyes gleamed as he watched me lean against Kron's bare chest, making him witness me tilting my head back and rubbing against the massive erection pressed between my asscheeks. Like a cat purring for her milk, I relished it when Kron banded his arm around my waist and held me to him, a low rumble in the back of his throat stroking up my spine like his touch had earlier.

His lips brushed against my temple. "Let me wash up. Arctok will take care of you."

"Yes, I will," he said as I stepped out of Kron's arms and into his.

My eyes fluttered shut as he bent down and covered my lips with his, followed by slow and drugging kisses. He stole my breath, hands sliding over my hips, up my sides, thumbs brushing tantalizing circles against the sides of my breasts.

Did I want this? God yeah. Now that I had the three of them within arm's reach, naked and wanting me, their silver eyes unable to tear away, I couldn't get enough. I reached up on tiptoe and curled my arm around Arctok's neck, meeting his kisses with fervent need, leg lifting as if to drape my thigh over his hip and rub myself against him. Every fiber of my being wanted them and the long day walking in the two suns had primed me for this decadent surrender to them.

"Enough," he bit out with a groan, tearing himself away. His chest rose and fell haggardly as he pulled back with a searing look that had my toes curling in the sand under my feet. "Terono."

I saw why he pulled away when he snatched the soap back from Terono and started scrubbing off. I was helpless to do anything but watch all those bulky muscles flex as he bent and scrubbed. Only when Terono put his finger under my chin and turned my head toward him did I tear my gaze away.

Then Terono's smirking lips looked too tempting to ignore. The asshole wanted me to pay attention, did he? Grinning, I slid my hand up his now-clean chest and satisfied myself watching his nostrils flare, a hint of uncertainty in his expression as I pushed myself up on tiptoe to brush my lips against his cool ones.

My other hand wrapped around his cock.

His mouth softened, a ragged moan ripping free as I tried to touch my fingers around his thick girth. Impossible, really, that they could all be so big.

"Is this too much teasing for you?" I murmured, smirking as he tensed under my hands.

He growled and this time it was him charging forward, leading the kiss with a ferocity that left me gasping into his mouth. Our tongues twined and he pulled, trying to tear out my soul through our connection. He was an aggressive kisser, all tongue and teeth, cruel in the way he wrapped my hair around his fist, and then soft, keeping me on the edge of pain.

Stroking his cock only fueled his madness, the beast restrained behind the cage of this arrogant alien. His shoulder bunched under my hand, his breathing ragged as I stroked him from base to tip, marveling at the velvet coldness of the thick ridges along the top of his cock ending in a curved, shovel-like head.

Terono groaned against my lips. "Please tell us you're no virgin."

"Not a virgin," I confirmed in a whisper.

"Thank whatever gods care," he murmured and took me in another hard, stinging kiss. My legs left the water the next instant when he grabbed me up. He swallowed my shriek, catching me under the ass as he lifted me to his chest and waded through the water toward the shore.

"She's got soap all on her back!"

Terono yanked back as I broke into giggles, though he carried me steadily up the bank. "It won't kill her."

"We'll just be squeaky clean," I agreed with him, nipping at his lower lip and then making a path down his jaw, nuzzling and tasting him. His fingers dug hard into my ass and he huffed a breath like he wanted to scold but didn't have the time for it.

He crossed to the spread out sleeping bags and sat, keeping hold of me so I wiggled in his lap, cool water clinging to us. Hands sliding up my back, he soaked me in with his gaze and I leaned back to let him, my own attention drawn to how good it looked to see my human skin against his silver-white skin, gleaming in the night. If not for his size and that demonic gleam in his eye, he might even be called ethereal.

Heavy-lidded eyes met mine when my gaze finally came up. "Like what you see, princess?"

The skin on my shoulders and down my arms pebbled. "I do," I said, the words coming out more breathier than I'd intended.

"Good," he growled, pulling me in for another kiss. Ravenous, devouring. He framed my face with his huge hands, holding me there as if I might escape. Holding me still so he could ravage the rest of my self control.

My hips moved, my sex sliding against his erection and spreading my slick arousal. I shifted up, lifting my ass off his thighs, and he froze against me as I lined up the head of his cock at my entrance.

I licked my lips, gathered my nerves. "Have you ever done this with a human?"

"No," he said, taking in my expression. Something softened in his hardened features. "But the Saitate are compatible with most of the universe. You'll be fine."

"And we won't hurt you," said Kron, sitting on his knees beside us, his kind eyes at odds with the raging erection gripped in his hand.

"Ready?" Terono asked as Arctok's heat arrived at my back, his chest pressing delicious heat through me. Terono's gaze flitted to him as he pressed an open-mouthed kiss against my shoulder, but he didn't say anything about the intrusion.

I nodded.

Bracing my heels on the ground behind Terono, I started the slow stretch of impaling myself on his cock. Lips parted, my eyes closed, a wrinkle forming between my brow as I worked myself down on him. He was unbelievably thick, like a fist lodged in the back of my throat.

"Oh, fuck, I—" I bit my lip, holding back the instinctive need to stop, rest, recuperate. He was barely inside me!

Sharp lines of tension dissected his neck as Terono let his head fall back. "Vekking tight."

I had barely noticed Arctok's lips butterflying around the base of my neck. But what didn't go unnoticed was his hand slipping between Terono and me, sliding against my clit. I gasped, holding onto his wrist as he coaxed me on. He grazed his teeth along my neck and it was Terono's turn to make a noise as I rocked my hips against him, misgivings forgotten. Pain was in the distance, now I floated in a wake of sublime pleasure.

"Do you *ever* end?" I gasped to their general amusement. He went on forever. I celebrated every inch I took of him but I wasn't anywhere near done. Arctok's free hand curved over my waist, his hot breath brushing my ear.

"Feels good to be on his cock, huh? Finally make him shut up—"

"Shut up," Terono grunted.

"Use him to sate yourself, Natalie. Torture him with that tight little cunt." He flicked my clit, driving spikes of pleasure through me, and his own breath caught as I clenched around Terono. "Stars above, you feel like a goddess."

I panted, a whine at the back of my throat. "I don't think I'll fit all of him."

"Nonsense. Slow and steady will do it," Arctok said, and he sounded so sure, so confident, that my shoulders relaxed. He squeezed my hip, using a smidgeon of his strength to push me down a couple more centimeters. "Can you rock into her a little?" he said in a tight voice.

Terono grinned a macabre, frozen grin. "I don't think I can *move* without exploding."

"He didn't ask about your stamina," Kron said. He shifted forward until he filled my vision. Silver eyes held the universe and I drifted into his gaze. They held me there as he framed my face with his hands, as his mouth caught mine up, his tongue sneaking into my mouth and stealing my taste from me. Arctok skimmed his mouth across my shoulder and used his hands to caress me everywhere, flicking my nipples with his thumbs, trading between light and hard touches until I was squirming again.

There was sensation everywhere, so much, so much, and my hips rocked and Terono started thrusting. Lightly at first, testing how far he could slip into me, and then harder as I held onto Kron's shoulders.

When we finally did it, all four of us groaned.

Kron leaned back, lazy satisfaction lighting up the gleam in his eyes. He bit his lip as he took the three of us in. "Good girl."

Shifting tugged at the heart of our joining. Their inhuman connection was no more better demonstrated in how that simple movement affected them all. Terono gasping and slamming his eyes shut as if I had put him on the rack, Arctok hissing next to my ear, Kron clenching his hand in the sleeping bag until his knuckles turned pink.

My eyes grew heavy with pleasure. Power was addictive. Having the three of them under my spell with one swirl of my hips... it should be illegal.

Terono was lodged in the back of my throat. It should have been impossible to move, but I could. Stretched out, impaled on him, I waited for the pain. But besides an edge of discomfort riding the motion, I could ride him without feeling like I was split in two.

And did I want to ride him! Those ridges along his cock were doing amazing things to me, fireworks exploding in my eyes with each slow rise and fall. Some of these dark places were so far unexplored until now and I shuddered with ecstasy as he pressed against them.

Then my eyes shut and I got a glimpse of...

"What is it?" Terono asked when I cried out. He gripped my hips so hard I'd carry his touch on me in the morning.

"It's-" I shook my head. "I don't know."

Arctok brushed his hand up my spine. "Did you see something?"

"I think so." I swallowed. It hadn't been real, had it? But there was understanding in Arctok's voice and rising realization in Terono and Kron's expressions. I closed my eyes again and it was there still, the silvery blue image like a painted dream, a running river, a feeling like wonder and pleasure not unlike my own rippling and racing across the connection, with masculine pride running like a gold streak underneath it all.

Arctok's gentle voice brought me back to the world at present. "When a Saitate covey mate, there's a chance of entering our bond, if only for a time."

My brow furrowed as I concentrated on the connection. "I feel... I feel myself. Around me."

I gave an experimental roll of my hips and the pleasure doubled, that achingly good restriction rocketing up my spine at the same time it did theirs. My mouth dropped open, panting as I realized I was fucking myself while I fucked... while I fucked *them*. Because it wasn't just Terono's cock I was sitting on, it was Arctok and Kron's too, at least from how they felt it through their connection.

Holy shit.

My climax hit, breaking through all of us in wave after wave as I clenched around Terono, as Arctok's balls seized up, as Kron bit at my lips. Leaning forward, I laced my hands at the back of Terono's neck, the phantom afterimages of my sweat-soaked skin pressed against his echoing in my mind, holding on as I broke again on the ridges of his cock. It felt too good, drowning underneath the tidal waves of feeling, filled to the brim with pleasure like liquid in a glass about to spill over the lip of the glass.

I grabbed at Kron's chest. His hot breath ruffled my temple as my hand slid down his chest, over the contours of muscle, until I wrapped my hand around the base of his cock. Ripples shuddered through all of us, and Terono tightened his grip as he ground into me. I wanted—*needed* some physical anchor to hold onto, stop me from drifting into the current of their connection.

Kron was only too happy to provide, his groan starting in his throat and ending in Arctok's. He thrust his cock into my hand, his hand wrapping around mine and guiding me up and down his large shaft, seemingly pleased by the sloppiness of it as I lost the battle with this new stimulation.

I don't have a cock, I told myself.

And yet. And yet.

Surreal images flickered across my mind, some of them too fast to comprehend. Arctok driving into me from above. My flushed face as I gasped out their names. Lips wrapping around Kron's cock. We were all undone, their fantasies melding into my mind as I rode Terono's cock. And under it was a feeling, something tinged with awe for this goddess who took them in.

"Come for us," Arctok murmured, his swirling fingers at my clit jolting me out of my haze.

I did. Again, my spine arching back as it hit me, the lightning strike of their pleasure spiking hitting me in the stomach. Terono seemed to grow even bigger, solid, a battering ram filling me. Fingers dug into my hips and brought me screaming down on him as he shot ropes of hot seed deep inside me.

"Vek!"

I cried out as he bit down on my shoulder, the pain of it making me clench and writhe on his lap. Warmth splattered against my back, hands roughly grabbing my breasts as Arctok slid his cock through the vestiges of his own release. Kron's hand tightened around mine, his cock swelling so much as he reached climax, I could barely grip him.

Eventually, we collapsed to the ground in a heap. Their connection released me with a sigh and I was back in my own mind, with only my own sensations and thoughts to occupy me.

"Hey," Terono murmured, his drowsy voice annoyed as I wiped my sticky hand against his chest.

"Sorry," I said, not sorry at all. If I was going to be covered in their seed, they could handle it too. Turning my head, I pressed a kiss to his chest and he grumbled, but didn't protest anymore.

Kron, his expression one of supreme satisfaction, caught my eye as he rolled onto his back beside us, arm under his head. He caught me looking and winked. "You stayed in longer than most."

"What a rollercoaster. You could've warned a girl."

"Sorry," Arctok said from my other side. My sweat-slicked hair stuck to my face as I turned to look at him. "It doesn't hit everyone the same."

"At least I know you guys enjoyed it."

All three of them tensed as I shifted atop of Terono, who held my hip. "A few more minutes," he said, sounding more awake now. "To let the swelling go down."

I laid my head back down on his chest, not feeling all that bothered as their release dried on my skin. In a way, it was perfect. His huge cock acted like a plug to keep me filled, and I dreaded the mess that would ensue when he moved.

I sighed. "I totally didn't wash my clothes."

Terono's smirk was in his voice. "That's all right. We still like you when you smell like fish."

9

"Here we are. The Hub," Kron said as we stopped at the mountain overhang overlooking the city. The sunlight shone off the top of roofs and what looked like solar panels to my uneducated eyes. The buzz and hum of activity reached us about half a mile away, making me excited and speed up my steps, despite the pain glowing in my thighs. They had all cautioned me that it would be disappointing... and maybe it was, for those used to seeing alien settlements.

For me, it was worth a little excitement.

"It's called the Hub?"

"It has a fancier name, but no one uses it. It used to be the supply depot when this place was a prison," Arctok said, looking at me instead of the view. Kron and Terono had already halfway descended the little livestock path we were on, a path clinging to the edge of the mountain face.

I nibbled my lip as I watched them carefully descend, hands holding onto the wall for balance. It would be a pain in the ass to climb down myself, especially with all the excitement of the night before.

"Want to climb on my back?"

To my everlasting shame, the guys had been attentive all

day, noticing my struggle moving and offering to carry me or lift me on their shoulders. The heat on my face now was definitely because of my embarrassment and not the two suns.

I grimaced instinctually at the thought of stretching out my thighs. "I think I can manage. It's only a little ways."

I ached by the time we crossed into the Hub's limits.

"Another one?" Terono asked as Kron returned from the last pilot left on the docks. The pilot and some of his crew gazed at me openly as Kron rejoined our huddle at the edge of the platform where the spaceships landed and waited for passengers, if any were willing to pay the price.

Kron grimaced, glancing at me as if hating that I could over-hear this. "Yeah, unfortunately."

I slumped. "What *is* it with people wanting bed slaves? I guess I shouldn't be surprised. People everywhere are terrible, even in space."

Arctok squeezed my shoulder.

"What price did they offer for her this time?"

"Not a good one," Kron said with a snort.

"What!?" It blew my mind that the idea of being bought for a low price made me indignant. I should've been enraged about the idea of the guys selling me like I was some possession, and maybe I would have been if I thought there was any chance in hell of that happening. I stomped my foot and glared at the pilot and his men, who started laughing like a bunch of hyenas. Literally.

"With the crash, it seems like everyone is expecting a glut of human females to show up at auction soon," Kron said.

"Ugh, gross."

"And no one is thinking of bringing them home to Earth, at least no one here *now*. That might change as the seasons pass."

Terono reached over and squeezed my hand. My shoulders

slumped. That meant my opportunity to get home was less than a microscopic speck of dirt on my Chucks.

I sighed. "What now?"

Kron continued playing the voice of reason. "Well, with no one offering rides off the planet... your best chance is to wait it out until someone will."

"You can stay with us," Arctok said, a hint of excitement in his eyes. "We'll ride it out for a couple seasons—"

"—and contact the pilots we trust when the time comes," Terono added. "I disliked the idea of coming here now when we barely know any of these pilots anyway."

My heart swelled. "Aw, you guys. You've already done so much though—"

"We're not leaving you to fend for yourself," Kron said in a tone brooking no argument.

Arctok squeezed my hip. "You're our responsibility."

"Your burden, you mean," I muttered toward the ground.

"Chin up," Terono said, chucking me under the chin until I hesitantly met his eyes. "We'll fully expect you to pull your weight. You won't be a burden to us."

I dropped my eyes again. This time, it was to hide my own elation, a growing lamp glow of happiness burning in my chest. They wanted me to stay! Well, they hadn't exactly said they *wanted* that, but they were willing to put me up... and that meant exploring whatever this was I felt for them.

Fear and caution bubbled up, trying to distract me with thoughts of break ups and how they'd totally chain me up in a basement. I burst those bubbles as fast as I could. They were decent men—*males*. I could trust them.

I finally looked up, looking them all in the eyes. "You all are okay with that?"

"We are in agreement," Kron said solemnly.

Arctok bent down and pressed his lips to my hair. "Where you're concerned, we always will be."

Stop it! I told my heart, which wanted to slam right out of my chest.

I cleared my throat before bobbing my head. "All right. Let's do that then."

Kron clapped Terono and Arctok on their backs. "Good. Now... you two go haggle a transport home for us. I'll take Natalie for some clean clothes. We have a few favors to our name to spare."

We parted and Kron led me through the streets of the Hub. Coated in dust and in dire need of a good sweep, it still held a quaint charm to it. If not for the aliens of every shape and size, and the obvious weapons they carried holstered, or even in their hands as if poised to strike the first person to come near, I would have liked walking the streets a lot more. But beside Kron, I didn't feel unsafe.

Alien eyes saw him—weaponless, escorting a slip of a human—and they minded their own business.

We left the port area for a different one, this one filled with stalls and shops, people hawking their wares from tiny carts all the way to street-facing stores with windows for the window shoppers like me. The merchandise here made me itch for a credit card and a way to tote everything back home. Every-where I looked, I saw something I wanted to get my hands on.

A metal hair pin that would do your hair for you that did double duty as a voice-activated murder machine. A silky dress with form fitting bodice and pockets with little holders for poisons. Thigh high boots with metal stilettos. "Tested up to ten inches of flesh and bone," the shopkeeper told me when they saw me admiring the shoes. Kron quickly tugged me away.

There were quite a few things built to kill people, or at least maim, but there were other wares too. Beautiful pottery made on the planet with actual stardust ground into the paints. Jewelry that would make the biggest stars in Los Angeles scream with joy. Hanging sculptures looking like candy floss that flickered with contained lightning. There was so much, I didn't know where to look. The only issue was my stink.

"Should've washed my clothes," I murmured as another shopkeeper held their nose and shooed me away when I tried to come close.

"Soon," Kron said. He nodded to a stall up ahead. "The yellow one. The proprietor owes us a favor."

The proprietor, a small old woman with shiny black skin like polished rock, seemed to sigh when she saw us. Hunching over a cane, she pushed herself off her stool and over to the long table of goods behind her. She cracked a wizened, toothy grin at Kron as we approached.

"Kron. I hoped you were dead."

"You would make a terrible gambler," he replied. He put his hand on my shoulder. "This is Natalie. She needs a new wardrobe."

The woman looked me up and down and gave another grin. She had a lot of teeth, *a lot* of them. Like a shark's dental set in a chipmunk's mouth.

I never knew that *was a particular fear of mine. Holy crap!*

"Lucky you." She sniffed as she turned away to her table. "I never thought I'd have to repay what I owed. It's wrong of you to go and find some human mate and make me give you my wares free of charge."

"You don't like the deal, Hookin? We can take your cane back," Kron said, nodding to her thin cane. She clutched it tighter and he smirked. "It does me no harm to leave empty-handed."

Scowling, she snatched up a couple items from her table and thrust them at me. "Here. Your size."

"Oh, thank you. It's very pretty—"

"Yeah, yeah," she muttered, grabbing a bag and stuffing it full to the brim with a random assortment of clothes. "Try not to get your stench all over it."

"Uh, sorry." It *was* pretty bad, and I held out the dress and what looked like shiny tights away from my body. I grimaced. "Er, could I have some underwear too now? Kron, is there a place to get cleaned up here?"

"There's a place I can take you," he promised.

Hookin handed me a thin slip of fabric that looked two sizes too big. "Put it over your head and it'll conform," she said with a scowl at my reluctance.

No underwear? But I didn't want to ask the old shark mouthed alien and took the slip with a grateful smile.

"Go wash up," she snapped, shoving the bag at Kron. "And consider us even."

"One bag of clothes for a thin laser ejector that can cut off the arm of any would be thief, as you requested?"

"That's over four thousand credits in that bag!"

He weighed it in his hands. "Hm. We'll see. If we're not happy, we'll come back for the rest of our payment, Hookin."

She snapped all two hundred of her teeth at him. "Try it." Turning to me, she gave me a sinister look. "Do not put up with them treating my clothes terribly. I *will* know."

"Uh, yes ma'am."

Kron walked away with me at a steady clip, his arm casually thrown over my shoulders. His voice filled with amusement, he asked, "Why do I have the feeling you're more scared of her than anything else you've seen?"

"Because it's true," I hissed at his laughter.

Kron led me to the entrance of what he explained was a public shower where we could rent a private shower for a time period.

"Think you can burn my clothes?" I asked.

"I can get them cleaned," he said, with his smile stretching his full, kissable lips. Just looking at him made me bite the inside of my cheek, especially the way he was contemplating me back. He reached out, tugging the end of a lock of my hair. "What would you say to staying a little longer? Let us make some weapons to sell, and fund a ticket straight back to Earth..."

He paused and the air thickened around us as he gazed at me with pools of silver in his eyes. "You could stay with us longer."

My eyes widened. "You'd be okay with that?"

"More than. We like you, Natalie. We also know the perils of letting a good thing slip away."

A good thing. I liked that.

"What if I like it here so much I stay?"

I said it cheekily, expecting him to hem and haw, and butterflies exploded in my chest when he didn't so much as blink.

He grinned. "Then we'll have to find some work for you, I think."

We grinned like two stupid fools at each other for a moment, possibilities in the air around us. Unfortunately, Kron remembered himself for the badass alien he was and stopped grinning, but he still had that soft look in his gaze when he reached out and squeezed my waist.

"Throw your clothes out the stall. I'll stay out here and keep an eye out."

The shower came with a disposable bag of necessities and I spent a moment combing my messy hair to prepare it before stepping into the shower. I shoved my old clothes out of the stall and then spent a good long while in the shower. The water smelled weird and the soap smelled strongly of disinfectant, but this was no time to turn my nose up.

Once I was thoroughly clean, I stepped out of the shower and slipped on the thin scrap of fabric Hookin said would conform. It fell over my waist like water and then, just as she said, molded itself to my body, becoming stiff around my breasts and flexible at the waist. No panties to speak of, but I didn't mind going bare for a bit. Maybe that was the old crone's hint that I needed to get laid more.

The dress, however, would've made Los Angeles designers weep.

"I belong on the red carpet," I murmured, stepping out of

the stall. My wet hair in a braid over one shoulder, my Chucks on my feet, I looked a little odd in the robin's egg blue dress, but god, I looked *scrumptious*.

"I would totally do me," I murmured to myself in the mirror I found at the end of the row of cubicles. I turned to the side and inhaled. Yeah, this was definitely worth all the money.

"How pretty."

My gaze flicked behind me in the reflection. An alien with spines around her bald head gave me a cool smile. She had a female voice, and the way she stood exuded feminine confidence despite her blue skin and pointed teeth.

"Thanks," I said, grinning.

She appraised me again. "What a pity."

She moved lightning quick. A pinch on the back of my neck, my knees buckled. She banded her arm around my waist, catching me against her wiry body before I fell.

The only thing I saw was the silver syringe in her hand, expanding to overwhelm my vision.

Then I was out.

10

Waves. A gentle, soothing hush on the world. Reaching for me in the night.

Like home. Like the boardwalk at night when the people and tourists went home and you could finally hear the waves crawl up the beach.

I frowned. Something was missing.

Thump. Thump. Thump.

My eyes struggled to open. What—?

I grimaced, my mouth tasting like kimchi gone bad. "Ugh."

I wiped my tongue on the back of my hand. Tongue out, I froze.

The beach. There it was in the background behind me. Real, *present*.

Not a dream.

Da-dum-dum-thump.

Fear clogged my throat, making me dig my fingers into the sand beneath me. Sand. I was on the beach. And those were the cultists starting the drumbeat.

Didn't these fuckers understand the word *no*?

Footsteps in the sand drew closer. I turned my head, my stomach churning when I confirmed I was indeed with the cultists again. This one walked toward the beach with a stack of leaves. I could only follow him so far though. They hadn't tied me up—they had no need to. For some reason, it was impossible to move my legs.

They had dropped me underneath a tree before their awful ceremony, trusting the drugs to keep me compliant. I spit out sand as I tried to wriggle myself onto my stomach using only my hands. Compliant, my ass. There was no one near me, no one watching... now was the time.

Inch by inch, I dragged myself forward, using my forearms to dig into the sand and pull my dead body up the beach toward the tall grass. There was no destination in mind. Only *away*.

"Not again, sacrifice."

Hands grabbed me under the armpits and jerked me up. I screamed and tried to smack him, elbow him, do *anything*. Impossible.

This time, they tied my hands together and staked the rope into the ground. Even though it was sand, trying to tug up the stake only made me sweat and swear. Crap!

The cultist smirked down at me as I panted.

"Fuck you, you gangly freak!"

He gave me a mocking bow. "It's our honor to serve you."

"Yeah, serve me up on a platter," I said as he walked back toward the beach. A bonfire was going, and I let my head fall to the sand as its smoke wafted over to me and tickled my nose.

I could kill that spiny bitch. Everything was going *so* well. The guys were taking me to their compound. We could actually *explore* what was happening between us and maybe even sleep in a real bed. It wasn't fair that everything was going right for once after my arrival on this awful planet, and now I was back on the beach and being prepped to be a kraken's snack!

Hopefully, Kron didn't feel too bad. Well, he could feel a little bad. I *was* about to die.

Why hadn't I insisted we leave the Hub the first chance I

got? They were honorable, kind aliens, and I should've jumped at the first opportunity to go back with them. This world was cruel, but the weaponsmiths had done everything in their power to protect me even after all the trouble I caused them.

I sobbed and closed my eyes to everything but my misery.

A sniffling behind my back made me twist to see what it was. My lips parted. A hawni! That's right. I forgot I was human catnip to these cute things. Now, drawn to me for some reason, it nosed around me. I held very still until it sniffed the rope tying me to the stake in the ground.

"Chew it," I whispered to it. Its ears twitched, and it sat on its haunches to observe me. "Please," I whispered, glancing toward the bonfire where the aliens were. "Chew it before they come back."

The hawni lifted its head into the air and started keening. A screeching, piercing noise that turned every head within the area.

"Hey!" The nearest cultist started over. I glared at the hawni. "You jerk! This is about your friends, huh? This is revenge."

The hawni keened louder and then scurried away as the cultist drew near.

"Well, I'm *not sorry!*"

"Are you talking to that beast? Stupid sacrifice." The cultist sneered as he reached me and tore the stake out of the ground. He yanked the rope attached to my hands and jerked me a couple inches, making me splutter out the sand invading my mouth. He grabbed me by the elbow and roughly yanked me up. "No annoying weaponsmiths to get in the way this time. Our master will feed!"

My legs buckled under me. I noticed the raft sitting on the edge of the beach, water already lapping at its haphazard corners. They were going to sit me on that flimsy piece of wood that as sturdy as a toothpick and push me out!

Feeling was returning to my legs, pins and needles in my

feet and climbing up my shins. I resisted the cultist with everything I had, trying to break his grip, tugging back. Nothing. Immovable, the bastard grinned and tightened his grip as he dragged me along, leaving behind a long indention in the sand.

"Our master is hungry. Our master needs sustenance so he may provide for us—"

"Learn to eat sushi, you freak, and *not* sacrifice people."

The cultist stared down at me, unimpressed. His mouth opened.

An arrow *thwacked* into his chest.

It was a *thwack*. A powerful noise. An unforgettable noise to be remembered on long nights when I couldn't sleep. A piece of steel going through flesh and tendon and bones made an incongruously chipper sound.

The cultist looked down at the steel bolt embedded into his sternum. The end of the arrow, tipped with white feathers, ignited. A tiny blue and yellow flame danced on its tip and then raced up the arrow and toward the cultist.

I dove to the ground, landing face first as the fire reached the cultist and went up in a *whoosh*.

Annihilated. The fire touched him and he was just... gone. Burnt to a crisp in front of me. The blackened husk of his body fell to the sand, scattering black flakes of dead alien into the air. I gagged, the scent of burning meat searing into my brain.

"Grab her! Grab the sacrifice!"

The weaponsmiths. They were here! I fought as hands grabbed me, jerking me to my feet. Staggering, punching out, fighting the rolling of my stomach from the awful scene and the alien pulling me toward the beach, the raft waiting for their sacrifice. A chaotic mess, my slaps and kicks did nothing, my legs lacking all strength still, my arms weak against them.

"Call the master!" The new cultist's voice was a furious cry.

The attack had taken the drummer by surprise. He

fumbled with his sticks and shouted back, "He needs time to rise!"

"Call him NOW or it'll be us out there!"

Now *that* made things interesting. When the cultist jerked me again, I glared up at him. "Why don't you two feed it if you love it so much?"

His fingers dug savagely into my arm, making me cry out. "Shut up!"

The cultist hustled me to the raft. I looked around blindly. Where were they? I was staring in the wrong direction when another arrow whistled through the air and went through the chest of the cultist holding me. This one made a wet *shhhlck* noise as it sliced through him. I dived away from him, hitting the sand again and scraping my cheek.

His charred body hit the ground a few moments after.

At that point, I could've written a book about the noises an arrow makes as it killed someone.

"Get her, get AHHH—*yurkkkt.*"

"To safety!"

"The shore, fools!"

The cultists ran about in confusion. The arrows hitting them in the chest from unseen pursuers as they ran about like headless chickens didn't calm the chaos. One grabbed me and I came up swinging, finding my strength surging with my adrenaline. My guys were here, they were *here*, and I needed to get the hell out.

Another cultist, this one prepared to risk death for his master, grabbed me and shoved me toward the raft. But he was looking behind him, nervous and scared of the arrows killing his creepy mates, and I tore out of his grip. Seeing the water so close, nausea gagged me, the stench of the kraken embedded in my psyche.

There was only one way to deal with fear like that. I turned and kicked the cultist in the shin. He bent over shouting and I brought my knee up into his face.

"That's three hours of Crossfit a week!" I yelled and ran.

The bastards had torn my dress. *And* there was a crispy alien smudging it. My mind filled up with these thoughts as I ran away from the bulk of the cultists, now drawing away from the beach and their sea monster, toward the safety of their compound walls.

A hand grabbed my arm and nearly jerked me off my feet. I swung instinctively—and only as my body spun toward the person did I see them materialize in front of me.

My fist smacked into a silver shoulder. Lips parting, I gawked up at the alien in front of me, the last vestiges of his invisibility shield falling away.

"What a greeting, princess," Terono said with a smirk.

"Terono!" The huge alien took a step back, a grunt escaping him when I launched myself at his chest. He was stiff under my hands, and then he chuckled overhead and relaxed minutely, his arms wrapping around me in a tight hug that squeezed my breath out of me.

"Hello, princess. Are you tired of being fish bait?"

I pulled back, grinning. "Eh, it's all right. Look, they're all running off now! I guess they don't want to sacrifice me anymore."

"Sometimes insanity *can* be cured," Terono said.

The cultists ran across the sand, slipping and sliding in the mad rush to reach the tall walls of their compound. They didn't care about grace or each other. One cultist fell to the ground after one of his mates shoved him in the path of an arrow. Anything to get out of the path of the invisible enemies raining down immolation arrows on them. Getting their pet a snack was the last thing on their minds now with the scent of burned flesh in the air.

I scanned the air and the beach, searching for Arctok and Kron, but they were hidden obscenely well by their invisibility tech. Terono motioned to the paddleboard underneath him. He'd been part of the air assault then. "Need a lift?"

I grinned. "I do. What about Kron and Arctok?" A part of me worried they might get hurt even with their invisibility tech, but Terono would get huffy if I said so, so I kept my mouth shut.

"They'll stay here and take care of the clean up," he said. "You're stuck with me for the time being."

I couldn't stop grinning. "And you're stuck with me, so I think that's fair."

"You're our mate," he said, and his matter-of-fact manners made my heart do cartwheels. "You mind?"

Terono didn't wait before he picked me up, bridal style. Simultaneously, his paddleboard rose into the air, making my stomach do somersaults. I clung tight to him, clenching my eyes shut.

Terono rumbled in amusement. "So you'll knee a Moxic in the face, but you can't stand heights."

"Call it a fear of the ground," I said. Trying to take my mind off it as we lifted higher, the air playing with the hem of my dress so it tickled my legs, I cast around for something to ask. There was so much I wanted to know. How did they know where to find me? Did they kill that spiny bitch—or at least torture her a little? How did they get here so quickly?

And would they let me try out this invisibility tech of theirs?

But I couldn't stop myself peeking over his shoulder. Up high, *not* in the tentacle of a kraken but instead in Terono's secure arms, I could almost enjoy the land spread out behind us. The beach behind us, the ocean spreading its vast girth across the expanse, sunlight glinting off in the distance, creating a gold glow I couldn't see past. Black smoke drifted from a spot by the shore.

Turning my head, I held my hair back with one hand and turned away from the past. Onward to the future.

11

"See that? That's our compound."

"We're here already? It's so close to the cult." I shivered, not entirely from fear. The day may've been warm, but the constant wind went straight through my bones.

He sounded amused. "Do you doubt us? You shouldn't. What you don't see are the protections in place."

The smirk in his voice made me peel open my eyes and look up at him. "They'll stop the cult if they come?"

Now his smirk turned into a sly, cruel smile. "Oh, Arctok and Kron are making sure they won't bother you again."

I hesitated and the wind whipped my hair out of my hand. "You'll kill them?"

"Better. As soon as we got back here, we sent a comm to the various lenders on the planet. We collected their debts." Seeing my expression, he added, "We find one drop of sacrificial oil on them and we'll own everything they have. Turns out, they owe *a lot*. We may love a good fight—but we love investments more."

My eyebrows rose. "That's the evilest thing ever."

"It's a bad world out here. Sure you want to stay?"

We touched down on the ground, a landing as gentle as our departure. Terono bent down to set me on the ground, keeping his hands on my waist to hold me steady. My legs wobbled, but I held my weight. His touch lingered a moment longer before he stepped back and picked up his paddleboard.

"What's that thing called anyway?"

He shrugged the heavy board under his arm. "An aeroboard, princess. We'll have to get you used to all sorts of things, I see. Have you ever seen a house before?"

I rolled my eyes. "Of course I've seen a house. Jerk," I muttered, turning away. If he wasn't so damn hot and hadn't saved me three times now, and sizzling hot—and did I mention hot? Anyway, I would be pissed.

But my annoyance faded as I looked upon their compound.

A short brick wall ran the length of the outer perimeter, crawling with creeping vines, with tiny flowers struggling for life interspersed at the base. Red brick led up to the front of the house, bisecting a rock lawn with a foot tall water fountain. The house itself was something out of an architecture magazine, pulled straight from a clifftop in Spain. Stucco walls, sweeping archways with the deep shade underneath tantalizing whoever caught sight of it.

I gazed at it in wonder as Terono led me up the path.

"You guys didn't say you were rich."

Terono laughed, one of the few genuine laughs I had heard escaping him. "We're rich," he said. He pointed down a path to the side tracing its way around the house. "Our workshop is beyond that tree. That way is the pool."

"You have a *pool?*" Holy crap, aliens were fancy.

"It's heated by the hot springs flowing underneath the house," he said, gesturing to an imaginary path he could only see. "We have spent a long time developing this land. We were accustomed to much more on our home planet."

"Wow," I murmured, as he led me on.

Terono continued the tour once we were inside, showing me through a large living space with an expansive kitchen. A huge stove big enough to fit a whole hog took up one section of the space. A sunroom was set aside for artistic pursuits, and Terono had to tear me out of a rec room with a holographic video feed and some kind of ping pong table that I couldn't comprehend at first glance.

Their space gleamed, every surface spotless and sometimes sparkling. Someone was obviously a clean freak. It was a lived-in space by three men profoundly comfortable with themselves and their lot in life, with little to no worries.

"What do you think?" Terono asked as we returned to the middle of the ground floor in front of a tiled staircase leading to the second floor. He bounced on the balls of his feet, his expression surprisingly nervous for such a confident male.

"Up there are the bedrooms?" I asked, ignoring his question for the moment.

He blinked. "Uh, yes. One for each of us and room for guests."

"Guests," I said, tapping my chin. "Is there one with a really *big* bed?"

His gaze flicked to the door and then back, turning a scheming, narrowed look on me. "I think we can find something," he said with a smirk tugging the corners of his lips. "How about we go find it now—" He cut off with a burst of laughter and a shake of his head.

I stared at this strangeness. "What did you just do?"

"It's not what *I* did, but what my other covey mates did," he said, straightening with a smile lingering in his eyes. "They don't take kindly to my plan."

His plan? Oh. My eyes widened. Right, the whole connection between the three of them, feeling what they felt. Not good when they needed focus.

But there would be so many opportunities to mess with them otherwise! Keeping my evil thoughts at bay, I smiled regretfully at Terono. "I suppose it would be distracting in a fight."

"Very," he said. "Or in flight. They are returning now.

Come, we will stay down here and pretend to be thoroughly platonic for their sake."

"Does me making tea sound thoroughly platonic? Wait—do you even have tea? Is tea a thing here?" Horror washed over me. What would I do without my chamomile tea in the evenings? My peppermint tea around my time of the month? Oh god, living in space would be *horrible*—

"We have tea," he said with an amused rumble.

"Oh good. What about medicinal teas?"

Okay, I'd admit it - I was a terrible tea snob. There was one thing I noticed about the people in LA, they picked one 'strange' habit by midwestern standards and kept at it. Mine happened to be tea.

Terono snorted. "You and Arctok will get along like water on a taxihl."

"I'll take that as a good thing."

We moved to the kitchen and Terono watched me browse through the tea selection. What the labels said, I had no idea, but the scents that escaped the jars when I opened them were *amazing*.

"This is perfect," I murmured.

"I'm glad you approve," Arctok said as he entered through the side door, Kron at his heels, tracking sand into the house.

I smiled, opening my mouth to say something when Kron took me by surprise. He pushed past Arctok and swept me up, tea jar and all, and then we kissed, furious and desperate, my ass hitting the cold countertop as he sat me down on it, his grip on my hips making me arch and curl toward him.

He pulled away and we gasped for a few moments in silence, foreheads pressed together, his gaze like a prayer answered.

"I'm sorry I lost you."

"It's okay," I whispered. Now that I was breathing again after that breath-stealing kiss, I made a face and looked down at my hands, now covered in grime I didn't want to think about. "You're covered in guts. I didn't think you were killing them."

Kron straightened, brushing my hair off my shoulder in one final sweet act. "We chopped off a couple pieces of that fish in your honor."

"Reminded them who they really need to worship," Arctok said, nudging Kron away so he could steal a kiss of his own. I grinned against his lips. So casual, and yet so right, fitted between the two of them with Terono nearby.

Kron snorted. "Also, it came up looking for its meal after those idiots stopped playing the drums. It nearly killed us."

"You're too forgiving of him," Arctok said, sliding a narrow eyed look at Kron with a glint in his eye, echoing his teasing grin. "That fish didn't wallop him enough, in my opinion. He should suffer more for losing you in the Hub."

I tickled his hard stomach as he slipped between my knees. "Hm, would it help if I demand lots of orgasms?"

"Yes," the three of them said at once.

Arctok leaned into my hand, going in for another kiss—

His eyes widened when I slapped my other hand down on his chest.

"But first, baths. We've smelled like fish long enough and I really don't want to develop a kink for sushi."

Arctok gave me a slow, sly smile that simmered under my skin. "We can do that."

I jumped up and down excitedly as I finished my lap. "I did it! I did a whole lap!"

The next moment I had to throw my arms out and grab hold of the side of the pool before I lost my balance when underwater. These aliens did not know how to build a shallow end.

Arctok stood serenely against the wall of the pool, indulging me on the warm afternoon with nothing else to do. "You did passable," he said with a snort.

I rolled my eyes. "You have high standards. I don't plan on swimming in the ocean. Just this nice, heated pool."

He smirked. "No swimming with the kraken, then?" They had taken over my name for the giant sea creature with some enthusiasm.

"None whatsoever. I don't plan to be his snack, thank you. I'm no one's snack except yours."

"You humans and your saying," Arctok rumbled, but in a pleased way as he watched me awkwardly swim across the pool to him. I still wasn't the best with water and I think I could be forgiven for that. It only took one time being sacrificed to giant monster to tell me I was never going to be an Olympic swimmer. I was just happy that I could swim around the pool with minimal fuss.

Arctok eyed me as I closed the distance between us and his lips spread into a slow grin when I collided with his chest.

"You're up to something."

He looked way too kissable. His chest rumbled pleasantly as I rubbed my hand over his smooth, warm chest. I batted my eyes at him. "You know, teachers on Earth give out gold stars when students do a good job."

"You want a star?"

I rolled my eyes at his raised eyebrows. "It's a sticker, not a real one."

"And what do I get in this exchange?"

"Hm... my love and affection?"

"I get those already," he said, unable to keep himself from touching me, studying me idly as his hands landed on my hips. His thumb brushed over my gently rounded belly. Yeah, alien birth control? Not a thing for the Saitate, apparently. Saitate had super sperm, because of course they did.

Not that I minded being baby trapped. Or being pampered like a queen by my three steadfast, hunky aliens. There was talk of making things official with the covey, ceremonies and maybe even risking a trip to their home planet to meet the fam, but we weren't in any rush. Life on Reazus Prime with my weaponsmiths was pretty laidback and right up my alley.

I tilted my head, a giddy schoolgirl feeling in my stomach when Arctok's gaze caressed my exposed throat. "What do you want in exchange then? I'm sure I can think of something."

"I think we should make this trade in my favor," he said, his husky voice making a shiver climb up my spine. I bit my lip and his playful gaze sparked. "But perhaps I can be persuaded."

Heavy footsteps and then a huge splash announced Kron. Water went everywhere. Our little petting session ended prematurely as I squealed and ducked away from the enormous splash.

Kron whipped his long hair out of his face as he rose from the water like some god straight out of the myths. His grin made it hard to be mad at him. "And how is our mate today?"

"Soaking wet," I said with a glare at him, pushing my soggy hair out of my face. Nothing like looking like a drowned rat in front of my boyfriends.

He hummed, careful as he approached to avoid my elbow which I was considering putting into his chest for that little stunt. "I believe Arctok was partially responsible for that."

He crowded me against Arctok, not shy as he curled his hands over my rounded belly. My anger bled away as his face softened with wonder. "How is my daughter today?"

I relaxed into him, letting my head fall back to his chest as I rubbed my hands over Arctok's forearms. "Enjoying having the three of you home all day."

He grunted in agreement. "Not as much as I enjoy being home."

"So no more heads to bust?"

"No more cultists to bother us," Arctok assured me. With a smirk, he added, "They were really attached to that sacred oil you drank."

I made a face. Having the last of the cultists gone was worth their absence for a while. The guys had taken shifts as they hunted down the last of the cultists after a kidnapping attempt almost got me. Now, nearly a full year later, we were finally free of the threat, and I could have their full attention again.

"Now about those stars," Arctok said as his hand drifted over my hips.

Kron was on the same wavelength, and he took pleasure cupping my breasts. I hissed, my heavy breasts growing sensitive every day. "Hurt?" he asked, worried.

"No, it feels good," I said as I raised my arm and hooked it over Kron's shoulder.

"Good. What stars are we talking about?" He took advantage of my exposed neck, nibbling and biting down the length of it, tending to the desire pooling between my legs. "Are these the stars you'll see as you slide over my cock?"

Water lapped at our sides, but nothing could compare to the heat of them. I wanted to sink into them, let them take me wherever they wanted. We could spend all day and night in bed and I still couldn't get enough. My hand drifted down, and I relished Arctok's groan as I cupped his hard cock. My guys didn't believe in swimsuits and, oh boy, did I love taking advantage of that.

Inside, there was a shout, followed by a string of curse words too niche for my translator to interpret.

"Um...? What was Terono working on?"

"Something with a lot of small pieces, I think," Kron said, and muffled a laugh into my neck as Terono's stomping footsteps thundered out to us.

A moment later Terono appeared in the backdoor like a thundercloud. *Someone* laughed—definitely not me, for sure, nothing funny about a silver alien with a huge singe mark across his eyebrows. "I am *working*," he snarled at us, seething.

Arctok shrugged without a hint of concern. "Then stop." He curled his hand around mine and we both watched Terono struggle as he used my hand to slowly pump his cock. "Our lustful mate needs to see stars."

"I'm not lustful," I said, breaking off with a moan as Kron flicked his thumbs across my hard nipples. The three aliens scoffed.

"You can barely finish a swim lesson without climbing one of us," Kron argued. "One lap and you're ready to crawl into the sheets. What else would you call that besides needy?"

"Maybe I like climbing better than swimming."

Terono growled as he stalked toward us across the patio, shedding his shorts and shirt as he came. "You need to time your voracious appetite better, princess."

"Mm, I'll try," I said, licking my lips as he sank down into the pool. Okay, so maybe a *little* lustful. But there was no helping it when my silver hunks were nearby.

Arctok pulled the strings of my bikini, and I let my mates satisfy my cravings.

MORE OUTLAW PLANET

Do you like steamy RH with alien and supernatural heroes who will fight their way across the galaxy for the female they've claimed? Sign up for my newsletter at cadyaustin.com to get the latest news about my new releases.

Like this? Do you want more Outlaw Planet?

Thanks for reading about my alien outlaws on Reazus Prime! You can find more hunky outlaws, pirates, and heroes in the rest of the series.

Cherished Galaxy Series

Diamond Girl

Serials

The Source Queen - Kindle Vella and Radish

Succubus Southern Nights (complete) - Radish exclusive